BRIE'S SUBMISSION

Her Sweet Surrender

Red Phoenix

Copyright © 2021 Red Phoenix
Print Edition
www.redphoenixauthor.com

Her Sweet Surrender:
Brie's Submission Book 21

Cover by Shanoff Designs
Formatted by BB Books
Phoenix symbol by Nicole Delfs

Dedication

I dedicate this book to my father.

While writing this book, my father passed away unexpectedly. It was a great shock and I had to push back the release to deal with my grief.

Although my father never read any of my books, he was proud of me and was amazed by my fans – who are the best fans in the world.

To my fans, thank you for your patience and encouragement. You will never know how much your support meant to me during this time. I hope Her Sweet Surrender means as much to you as it does to me.

I'm sure that it won't come as too much of a shock when I say that Brie's father is loosely based on my dad. So, he will continue to live on in my stories and that brings me comfort.

Many thanks to Penny Reid for her help as a friend when I was struggling.

As always, I must thank Kh Koehler, editor and friend. She has my back, no matter how crazy it gets!

A deep thanks to my dear betas: Becki, Brenda, Maryiln and Kathy.

My marketing team, Jon and Jess. I am grateful for every day I get to work with you.

Thanks to these peeps for sharing a Lea joke that was chosen from my FB group, Friends of Red Phoenix: Rebecca Cadwallader, Heather Rakowski, Shirley Parrott-Copus, and Michael Beaudet

Last, but never least, MrRed. You have been so patient, gentle, and kind while I grieve for my father. Thank you for remaining by my side and loving me through good times and bad.

SIGN UP FOR MY NEWSLETTER
HERE FOR THE LATEST RED
PHOENIX UPDATES

FOLLOW ME ON INSTAGRAM
INSTAGRAM.COM/REDPHOENIXAUTHOR

SALES, GIVEAWAYS, NEW
RELEASES, PREORDER LINKS, AND
MORE!

SIGN UP HERE
REDPHOENIXAUTHOR.COM/NEWSLETTER-
SIGNUP

CONTENTS

Surprise! 1

Happy News 9

Payback 22

The Rose 40

Heated Exchange 55

Toying with Her 70

Firsts 82

Slaying Them 94

Precious Gifts 104

Returning Home 118

Blessed Event 136

Kylie 153

Tribute 166

Confessions 176

Kindness 187

The Plan 198

Cuffed 207

This Moment.. 220

Bonus Content.. 227

A Condor's Birthday 228

Coming Next.. 231

About the Author.. 233

Other Books by Red Phoenix........................... 237

Connect with Red on Substance B 243

Surprise!

B rie lay on the sandy beach while Sir meticulously combed her hair out with his fingers so that her long locks framed her face like the rays of the sun.

"Don't move," he ordered once he was done.

She smiled, looking up at the bright blue sky. Practicing a little objectification, Brie pretended she was a platter of sunshine. She didn't move a muscle as she watched a lone cloud slowly float across the Italian sky, while listening to the waves gently crashing against the shore.

This is pure heaven…

Brie always enjoyed revisiting the tiny island Sir and his father had unofficially claimed when Sir was a boy. It held a special place in her heart knowing how much it meant to him.

But they had created their own memories here, as well. She would never forget the day they discovered the chest, buried for years, waiting for Sir to open it.

Brie closed her eyes, recalling the feel of the expensive Italian wine rolling off her breasts as Sir poured the red liquid over them and then licked it from her nipples.

1

He had then poured the wine over his rigid cock and commanded her to suck it.

She let out a contented sigh.

Brie could still remember the musky berries and vanilla flavor that made up the Brunello di Montalcino wine. It mixed with Sir's maleness as she ran her tongue over the length of his cock.

Memories...

"Good girl," Sir growled seductively upon his return.

Lying beside her, he began placing the shells he'd just collected in a decorative pattern in her hair. When he was finished, he sat back to gaze at her. "My beautiful goddess..."

Brie smiled as he leaned down to kiss her. Her mind must have been playing tricks on her because she swore she tasted the wine on his lips.

"You taste delicious, Master..." she purred.

He pressed his lips against hers again more firmly this time, claiming her mouth with his tongue. Brie's heart fluttered, her whole body responding to the possessive kiss.

A loud crack, like the sound of a breaking tree, echoed from the other side of the small island, interrupting their intimate moment. They looked toward the sound as a flock of startled birds flew into the air near its location.

"I wonder what that was," Sir mused, pushing himself back off the ground and getting to his feet. "Stay here while I check. I don't want you ruining my creation while I'm gone."

Brie dutifully lay there, delighted to be his piece of art. However, after several minutes, curiosity got the best of her.

Although it would lead to a punitive spanking, Brie

turned her head slightly to see if he was returning.

To her surprise, she saw three people in the distance walking toward her. A woman in a red dress flanked by two men. The bright sunlight made it difficult to make out their faces.

Her heart began to race as they drew nearer and she wondered if she should break protocol or if this was meant as a test. Brie fought with herself, denying her instinct to move. She realized her mistake the instant she recognized the woman's face.

Brie's blood ran cold when Lilly smiled at her.

"Surprise! I see the little sex slave is all prepared for her journey."

As Brie scrambled to her feet in terror, noticing the men beside her were Liam and his twin brother.

"How did you get here?" she whimpered, looking past them to search for Sir.

Lilly's laughter was cruel. "There will be no rescue for you this time, Brianna…"

Brie woke with a start, struggling to breathe.

She turned her head to see Sir sleeping peacefully beside her.

Although it was only a dream, Brie's heart continued to pound in her chest. The nightmare had felt so real and she had to fight hard to convince herself that everything was okay.

A lone tear rolled down her cheek as she stared up at the ceiling. There had been only one overriding thought in her dream once she realized Lilly had come to kidnap her.

At least Hope is safe.

Even in her dreams, Brie's mothering instincts overpowered every other thought.

"I'm okay," Brie whispered to herself, struggling to calm her urge to scream.

She knew her dream had everything to do with last night's meeting, so she replayed the conversation in her mind.

"I say we kill her and be done with it," Rytsar growled angrily. "I do not trust the creature."

There was rumbling among the others in attendance.

Brie shook her head. As much as she feared Lilly, she didn't want to be responsible for the woman's demise.

"I'm with Rytsar on this one," Mary stated firmly. "That woman has no soul. I've experienced it firsthand."

"I'm certain we can find a better solution—" Sir began.

"*Moy droog,*" Rytsar interrupted, "the creature wanted Hope dead and your wife enslaved. Do you really think she's changed? We spared her life once, but a snake has no concept of gratitude. Its only instinct is to strike its prey dead."

Glancing at Brie's stomach, Rytsar added, "Are you willing to risk their lives—and the babe yet to come?"

"There is a viable solution to any problem," Sir insisted. Looking around the room, he said, "It's the reason I called this meeting tonight. With so many great minds, I am certain we can come up with an effective plan to ensure Brie's safety."

Captain cleared his throat. "Although what Durov proposes is extreme, if we determine there is no other option, I believe it should remain on the table."

"There will be no discussion of murder!" Marquis Gray declared harshly.

Rytsar grumbled. "I understand you have *high* ideals, Gray. However, you do not know the creature as I do. If any harm comes to Brie or the children, it will lie squarely on our shoulders."

"We can't take that risk," Mary warned. "She's completely unhinged."

Marquis Gray stood up, frowning at the two of them. "I will not entertain the idea of killing the girl."

Rytsar snorted in disgust. "Do you remember when you insisted the authorities should handle her? What happened, Gray? The creature escaped from jail. If Wallace and I had not planned for it, Brianna would not be here. Eliminating the threat is the *only* option, as far as I am concerned."

Brie spoke up. "Since I'm the one facing Lilly's wrath, I have something to say."

Everyone turned to her, waiting for Brie to speak.

She glanced at Sir, who nodded his encouragement.

"We have to assess Lilly's state of mind before we make any decisions about her future. I personally believe people can change. I only need to look at myself to understand that." She smiled confidently at Sir. "I'm definitely not the same woman who walked into class my first night at the Submissive Training Center."

"Assess her how?" Marquis Gray pressed.

"Originally, I planned to join Sir and Rytsar because I wanted to see her in person." She unconsciously laid her hand on her stomach as she continued. "But, with the new baby coming, Sir and I have decided not to travel to Russia."

Glancing around the room, she added, "But I feel it

is important that someone join Rytsar."

"I volunteer," Mary immediately stated.

Brie looked at her in concern. "Are you sure?"

"Absolutely."

Sir shook his head. "No, you have endangered yourself enough where Lilly is concerned, Miss Wilson."

"I will go," Marquis announced. "However, the trip will have to wait until I finish the current training session."

"How long will that be?" Rytsar asked in frustration.

"We've just begun the second week, so about five weeks from now."

The Russian furrowed his brow. "Too long. This needs to be addressed now so we have time to formulate a foolproof plan."

"Agreed," Captain stated. "With Wallace currently indisposed, I should be the one to go. I can speak to my supervisor tomorrow and arrange the time off without any problem."

Brie appreciated Captain's military experience. She knew he had played an integral role in eliminating the Koslov brothers in Russia. It was easy to understand why Sir had chosen to include him. Captain was not influenced by emotions the way Rytsar was, and he understood the necessity for violence at times—unlike Marquis.

While Brie was comfortable with the idea of the two men assessing Lilly in her stead, Marquis voiced his concern. "It is imperative an experienced therapist evaluate her."

Rytsar's eyes narrowed. "What? You don't trust me?"

"It has nothing to do with trust and everything to do with professional experience."

The Russian looked to Brie. "Do you agree, *radost moya?*"

She had never considered it, but Brie liked the suggestion. "I think it will make the decision even clearer for me."

Sir nodded in approval. "An assessment from a certified therapist would give us vital information."

"Then I will arrange it," Rytsar declared. "And, there is only one man I would trust with such a task."

Marquis asked pointedly, "May I ask whom?"

"The highly respected Russian psychologist Mikhail Volkov. I've worked with him extensively in the past."

Captain spoke up, asking, "In what capacity?"

Rytsar's answer completely surprised Brie.

"He once headed a shelter I created for victims of sex trafficking."

"In Russia?" Brie asked. She knew about the one he'd set up in America, but she'd had no idea there were others.

"It is no longer running, *radost moya*," he explained. The sorrow in his voice left Brie to wonder what had happened.

Turning to Marquis, Rytsar added, "However, the groundbreaking program Dr. Volkov created is still being used in facilities throughout Russia."

"He's an excellent choice," Sir agreed.

Brie looked at Sir with interest. "Do you know Dr. Volkov?"

"I never met the man, but what he was able to accomplish at the shelter was impressive." He glanced at Rytsar. "I recall he unfailingly put the needs of the girls and the program above all else—even his own reputation."

"*Da*, that he did," Rytsar agreed somberly.

Brie appreciated learning something new about Rytsar's past because he was so closed about it. She was certain there was a much deeper story behind the shelter and the reason for its closure. She hoped someday he would trust her enough to share it.

"When do you want to leave?" Captain asked Rytsar.

"As soon as possible."

Captain nodded curtly.

Brie frowned, disappointed not to be traveling to Russia with them. "I wish I could go with you."

"It is important that you take care of yourself, *radost moya*." The Russian winked. "Be good and I will bring you back something special from Russia."

"All I want is you, maybe tied in a red bow?"

Rytsar burst out laughing. "Well, I'm certain I can do better than that."

Brie turned over in the bed trying to go back to sleep, but her heart would not stop racing. Eventually it became too much, so she slipped out of bed and made her way to Hope's room.

Leaving the light off, she quietly walked up to the crib and stared down at her child.

To her surprise, Hope was wide awake and reached for her. Brie smiled as she picked up her daughter and hugged her against her chest.

Immediately, a sense of peace enveloped Brie.

"We're okay," she murmured repeatedly, pushing the visions of Lilly out of her mind.

Happy News

B rie walked out of the nursery with Hope and headed downstairs.

She noticed her phone on the counter and immediately checked her messages, hoping to find one from Faelan. She was concerned about Kylie after Faelan rushed out of their home last night to meet her at the emergency room.

Brie hadn't heard a word since.

Although it was still early, she sent a short one-handed text.

How is Kylie?

She was surprised when he instantly texted back.

Kylie fainted at work. She's back home and is sleeping right now.

What happened?

I'll have her call you later. She should be the one to tell you.

Chills pricked Brie's skin when she read his text.

Is everything okay?

Everything is fine. Great in fact.

Brie let out a sigh of relief as she carried Hope to the

couch and sat down.

Don't scare me like that! she scolded.

Haha…no need to worry.

She wondered why he was still up if everything was fine but decided not to pry.

I can't wait to hear from Kylie.

I'll let her know that. BTW, how did the meeting go last night?

She shivered, still feeling unsettled by her dream.

Rytsar and Captain are heading to Russia to assess the situation.

I should have been the one to go with Rytsar.

No. Your job is to take care of Kylie now.

He paused for a moment before typing.

How are you handling this whole Lilly situation?

Brie didn't want to admit she'd had a dream about the woman, so she texted the words she'd been repeating to herself ever since she woke up from the nightmare.

I'm OK.

You know none of us will let her touch you.

I know.

Try to get some rest, blossom. You have a new baby on the way.

Brie smiled and glanced down at her stomach before texting. **You should get some sleep too.**

Will do.

Brie set the phone on the coffee table and lay down on the couch, placing Hope between her and the back of the sofa. She stared at her little girl, wondering what it was going to be like adding another child to their family.

"Are you going to have a little sister or brother?" Brie asked her, smiling as she tickled Hope's toes. The giggles that filled the room lightened Brie's troubled heart.

She suddenly got the chills, sensing a presence behind her.

Brie cried out in terror when she felt someone's hand on her, just before her mind registered the electricity of Sir's touch. Unfortunately, her scream startled Hope, causing her to cry.

"What's wrong, Brie?" Sir asked in concern as he picked Hope up to soothe her.

"I…" She swallowed hard as she sat up, embarrassed by her overreaction. "I had a bad dream. I'm fine, Sir."

"Was it a dream about Lilly?" he asked knowingly.

Brie nodded.

Sir sat down beside her, lightly bouncing Hope on his lap to keep the baby entertained. Still, his voice was somber when he asked, "Would you prefer it if I joined Durov on this trip?"

"No!" Brie wrapped her arms around him. "You are the only reason I can stay behind."

"What is it, then?"

She let go of him and sat back, shrugging as she tried to ignore her growing feeling of uneasiness. "Talking about Lilly brings up so many unpleasant memories." She sighed, smiling sadly. "It's kind of messing with my head."

Sir nodded thoughtfully. "I understand."

Brie gazed up into his eyes and noticed the pain he was trying to hide from her. She suddenly realized she wasn't the only one suffering.

Sir had never opened up about what happened to him in China. His journal was the only insight she had of that time he'd spent alone with Lilly. She'd memorized the entry Sir had written after reading it repeatedly while

11

he was in the hospital fighting for his life:

Babygirl,

My head still isn't right. I can't think, I can't eat, and my body won't stop shaking. I feel as if I've been poisoned. But, if so, it would be a poisoning of my own doing. It was meant to be a simple night of celebration at Lilly's insistence. Even I got caught up in her enthusiasm, partially hoping for her sake that she was right about Mother's recovery so I wouldn't have to see the devastation in her eyes when the scan came back proving the woman was brain dead.

You know I don't overindulge, but we did drink several concoctions at a local bar. How much and what they were, I can't say. The night quickly became a blur. I felt like a frat boy when I woke up in my hotel room the next day, unaware of how I had gotten there. More disturbing was the fact that my clothes were dirty and torn. Again...I have no recollection why.

Seeing my sorry condition, I stumbled to Lilly's room to check on her. She was slow to answer and in the same disheveled state. When I asked her about it, she only shook her head. It seemed her memory was as compromised as mine.

I wasn't able to go to the hospital that day as I felt too sick to leave my bed. Lilly told me she'd felt well enough by the afternoon to visit Mother and saw her eyelids flutter. Her false hope struck me the wrong way.

I guess it may have been the aftereffects of alcohol, but I lashed out. Whatever the case, I made the girl cry when I told her Mother would never recover because she's already dead. I didn't care that she refused to speak to me for the rest of the day. I needed time alone to recover.

That's when the dreams started. I was awakened repeatedly by nightmares littered with disturbing images and unholy screams. It's been two days, and I've still been unable to rest—and the shaking won't stop.

Lilly is overly concerned and has become highly attentive, trying to force herbal remedies and local soups down my throat. It grates on my nerves and I keep sending her away.

I want no one near me but you. However, I don't trust myself.

Babygirl, I seriously don't know what's wrong with me. I feel as if I have entered a black hole I won't return from...

Recalling those last words still gave Brie goose-bumps.

They now knew Lilly had accidentally given him an overdose, which almost killed him. However, Sir had had no idea he'd been drugged at the time. Brie could only imagine the horrors he experienced while he faced hallucinations he thought were real.

"How are you handling this, Sir?"

He shook his head, frowning. "It doesn't matter."

Brie reached up and caressed his clenched jaw. "It

matters to me."

"Protecting you is the only thing that matters, baby-girl."

She gazed deep into his eyes. "I'm not the only one who was hurt by Lilly."

Sir's frown deepened. "I'd rather not talk about it. It only stirs up memories that are best left in the past."

"But, Sir…" Brie began softly.

He glanced at her, saying nothing as he continued to bounce Hope on his knee.

She understood he wanted her to drop it, but she knew it was eating him up inside. "Holding all those feelings and memories in will only hurt you in the end." She added in a gentle voice, "Don't let Lilly have that kind of power over us."

Sir growled under his breath. "I have never been in a darker state of mind than I was in China."

Brie shivered, remembering how different he'd been when she arrived—so cold and remote, almost heartless.

"Even though I realize now the horrors I experienced were drug-induced, I haven't been able to forget them. At the time, it caused me to question everything about myself—and you."

Her bottom lip trembled. "I hardly recognized you when I arrived."

"I…" Sir closed his eyes, his voice tinged with anger and guilt. "I'm sorry for the way I treated you."

Although Brie had been hurt at the time, she felt overwhelming compassion for him now. "I didn't understand what was wrong, but I never doubted we would work through it."

"Always faithful," he stated with a sad smile.

"I'm completely devoted to you."

Sir stared at her, his gaze intense and unreadable. "I hope it doesn't become your undoing, babygirl."

"It won't," she assured him, but she could feel the intensity of his rage growing inside him.

Sir's lips curled into a snarl. "To be grossly manipulated like that by my own sister makes my skin crawl."

Brie shuddered. "I hate that she did that to you."

Sir turned away from Brie, stating in a far-off voice, "Not knowing what really happened still haunts me to this day. The screams. I will never forget the horrifying screams." His voice caught when he added, "I think they were mine."

A chill coursed down Brie's spine. She squeezed him tightly wishing she could turn back time and prevent Lilly from ever hurting him. "I'm so sorry, Sir."

He huffed angrily. "You are not the one who should apologize. I let my guard down and it almost cost you and Hope your lives."

"It isn't your fault. None of this is."

He shook his head, looking down at their daughter protectively. "I never should have trusted a product from my mother's loins. I knew better than that, but I—"

"You wanted a family. Everyone longs for that connection, Sir."

"It is a weakness. I failed to protect the person most precious to me because I was blinded by it. There is no excuse."

Brie squeezed him even tighter. "It is not a weakness, but a strength. I'm grateful that family means everything to you."

Sir grimaced. "Because of my actions, your life and those of our children continue to be threatened."

"I refuse to let Lilly have that kind of power over

us!"

"And yet, she does—even now," he replied coldly.

Brie shivered, leaning down to kiss Hope on the top of her head. It was true. No matter how much she wanted to deny it, she would always be afraid for Hope.

Sir's eyes flashed with anger. "It would be much easier to eliminate the threat and be done with her, but even that would not be enough for me." His voice turned icy when he shared, "I remember what she told Mary when she was at the Tatianna Legacy Center. When I think about her wanting to torture our daughter it makes me want to do unspeakable things to her. I *need* Lilly to suffer with the same intensity we have."

The severity of his hate was palpable.

She glanced at Hope. "It's natural to feel that way as her father, Sir. There's nothing wrong with it."

He stared at her, shaking his head slowly. The dangerous glint in his eyes became more ominous when he told her, "I am my mother's son, and Lilly brings out the worst in me."

His words chilled her to the bone.

Hope started fussing in his arms.

"You don't mean that, Sir."

"But, I do." He stared at her so intently that it frightened her. "In that way, she and I are very much alike."

Brie struggled to breathe.

While she understood why he wanted to hurt Lilly, if Sir were to do such a thing, she knew it would fundamentally change him. It would open the floodgates of his inner darkness, a darkness he held barely in check at times, and she feared there would be no coming back.

More than that, she would never be able to look at Sir in the same way again. It would create a rift so deep it would destroy them as a couple.

"Your sister is an inhuman monster, but you are not her," she insisted. "You are far too strong to let your inner demons control you."

She heard his sharp intake of breath and waited for his reaction, her heart beating rapidly in her chest.

Brie knew the two of them stood on a dangerous precipice. His instinctual need to protect her might become the driving force that would end up destroying him.

Hope began fussing in his arms again and started to cry.

Sir glanced down at his daughter. "Even my daughter can sense it in me." He tried to hand Hope back, but Brie refused to take her.

"Hope senses your inner struggle—nothing more."

He looked unconvinced but stood up and carried Hope to the large window overlooking the ocean. Rocking her in his arms, he murmured, "There, there. No tears, my little angel. Everything will be okay."

Brie knew Sir would never hurt the people he loved, and she wasn't afraid of facing his inner demons.

However, she was terrified those dark feelings he kept so tightly bottled would eventually end up ripping him apart. Walking up to them both, Brie put her hand on his back while wrapping an arm around Hope.

She could feel how incredibly tense he was. "I have a request, Sir."

He turned his head and stared at her.

"Talk to someone. If not me, someone you trust."

"Brie…" he muttered in protest.

"Please."

Sir growled under his breath but did not say no.

Despite his obvious displeasure, Brie was relieved that he was considering talking to someone. It was the only way he could work through those dark places he hid from the world—and himself.

Brie closed her eyes and laid her head against his chest.

We will find a way.

Her cell phone rang, breaking the heavy silence.

Brie walked over to pick it up, wanting to see who it was before she answered it. "It's Kylie, Sir."

"Good. We've been concerned about her."

Brie forced herself to smile when she answered the phone, wanting to hide the concern in her voice. "Hey, Kylie."

"Sorry to call so early, but Faelan said you were worried."

"I appreciate the phone call." She glanced at Sir. "We have been worried about you ever since Faelan rushed out to meet you at the emergency room."

"There's no need for concern," she giggled.

"Why? What happened?"

"I was filing some papers and felt a little woozy. Before I could sit down, I must have passed out because I woke up on the floor, looking up at all of my coworkers, who kept asking if I was okay. Funny thing is, I don't even remember hitting the ground. It was bizarre."

"What did the doctor say was wrong?" Brie asked her, still worried.

Kylie laughed. "That's the best part. Nothing is wrong."

"What do you mean?"

"I fainted because..." She paused for a moment. "I'm pregnant."

"Oh, my goodness, Kylie! What wonderful news—except for the fainting part."

She laughed. "It was the last thing we were expecting. It isn't as if we were even trying."

"So, when are you due?"

"I don't know yet. I need to make an appointment with an obstetrician. My periods have never been regular, so I don't keep track and have no idea when the last one was."

"If you're looking for a good obstetrician, I highly recommend Dr. Glas."

"Thanks! Text me his number when you get a chance. I'll check him out."

"Of course. This is so exciting, Kylie! Just think of all of the fun play dates we will have with our kids being so close in age."

She laughed. "I'm still trying to process the idea that I'm going to be a mother. I hope you don't mind me coming to you for advice if I need it."

"Not at all. I'll be happy to answer any questions you have."

"I can't believe I'm having a baby!" she cried, laughing.

"How did Faelan take the news?"

"It was adorable! He was so excited that he shook everyone's hand in the waiting room. Even though we had planned to hold off having kids a few more years, we're ready to start a family now."

"You're going to make great parents," Brie gushed. "When I think of the difference you've made in Faelan's life, and now this…he's lucky to have found you."

"I'm the lucky one," Kylie insisted. "I've been admiring that guy since high school and watched every football game he played in high school. I still have to pinch myself sometimes. The fact that I'm having his baby seems crazy wonderful to me."

"Well, there's no doubt you two were meant for each other," Brie said, grinning at Sir.

"I think so, too." Kylie giggled. "It was written in the stars."

"Who else knows your big news? I don't want to spoil your surprise."

"Just you and our parents right now. This is all too new for us. We're still kind of in shock."

"Well, I'm honored to be one of the first to know. I'm so happy for you guys!"

"Eep! I gotta go. Faelan just made me a breakfast fit for a queen."

Brie heard him in the background. *Can't let the woman carrying my child go hungry, now can I?*

"It's only 5:30 in the morning. I'm not even hungry yet," Kylie protested with a laugh before letting Brie go.

Brie smiled as she hung up. "Well, it looks like Faelan and Kylie are starting a family."

"Was that the reason for the trip to the emergency room?" Sir asked, letting Hope down to crawl on the floor. They both watched as Shadow suddenly appeared and bounded up to her, rubbing his head against her cheek. Hope filled the room with a happy squeal.

Sir chuckled as he walked to the couch to sit down. Brie joined him but chose to kneel at his feet, wanting to lay her head on his lap.

"Kylie fainted at work and scared everyone," she answered, then giggled softly. "Won't her coworkers be surprised when they find out the reason why?"

"I am happy for them both," Sir stated, staring at

Hope as she played with the cat.

Brie was grateful for the unexpected interruption. The happy news seemed to have put Sir in a better mood.

She purred softly when he began stroking her hair. "We will find a way through this, babygirl."

"I know we will, Sir."

Payback

B rie hadn't heard a peep from Rytsar for several days. It was unlike him not to call or drop by for a spontaneous visit. Then, on her morning walk down the beach, she noticed all the lights were off in his beach house as if no one was home.

Needing to know what was up, Brie decided to call him when she returned home.

"*Radost moya*, I can't talk right now," he answered curtly.

Hearing the seriousness in his tone, she immediately blurted, "Is everything okay?"

She overheard Captain's voice in the background. "There should be a turn up ahead on the right..."

Her heart began to race. "Are you in Russia?"

"*Da*, I am on the errand we discussed."

Brie's heart sank. "You left without telling us?"

He chuckled lightly. "I didn't want you to worry."

"Rytsar—"

"I must go, *radost*..." The phone call began to break up. "...we're out of range..."

"When can I expect you to call again?" she asked.

She was desperate not to lose the connection before he answered.

"We…"

Brie held the phone closer to her ear, hoping to hear his last words before the connection died completely. "…days until—"

The phone suddenly beeped twice, letting her know the phone call had been disconnected. She stared down at it forlornly.

"What was that all about?" Sir asked, walking out of his office.

"Rytsar already left for Russia with Captain."

"I was aware he wanted to leave soon but had no idea they'd left the country."

She sighed anxiously. "I wish they didn't have to go…"

Sir wrapped an arm around her. "This is simply a fact-finding mission. There is no reason to worry about either man."

Brie frowned. "I don't trust anything that involves Lilly."

"I happen to agree." Sir brushed his hand on her cheek tenderly. "Which is why I am taking your advice."

"Sir?"

"You were right when you said Lilly still holds power over me."

She looked at him in concern. "It's understandable, Sir."

Placing his finger on her lips, he told her, "No need to make excuses for me, babygirl. It is time I dealt with it. Although, if I am being honest, the prospect of it is terrifying."

She could only imagine how difficult it was for him

to face the betrayal and manipulation he'd suffered at the hands of his sister. She was grateful he was seeking help but had naturally assumed he would go to Rytsar since they were like brothers. However, with the Russian out of the country, she realized she had been mistaken.

"Is there anything I can do to help?" She felt a deep need to support him.

He nodded. "Actually, there is. Although I plan for it to be a private meeting, I would like you to come with me."

Brie was moved that he wanted her near. "It would be my honor, Sir."

"I'll make the arrangements then."

Brie wrapped her arms around him, knowing the courage it took to not only be vulnerable in front of another on such a deep and personal level but to face head-on the demons his sister had wrought.

Master Anderson surprised them with an unexpected visit a few days later. The moment Brie opened the door, she knew something was up because the sexy Dom was hiding something behind his back.

"Whatcha got there, Master Anderson?"

He took off his cowboy hat and was about to answer her, when Brie heard a muffled meow.

Master Anderson chuckled. "Guess the cat's out of the bag." He held up the cat carrier he'd been hiding.

Brie leaned in to see and was thrilled when she recognized who it was. "You brought Shadow's son Ghost Pepper?"

He winked. "I did."

Sir came up behind Brie and stared at the cat carrier, shaking his head. "No. Turn around right now and leave. I'm not housing another feline, no matter how much you beg."

Master Anderson brushed his hair back, laughing. "I wouldn't let you have Ghost if you paid me a million, buddy."

Sir eyed the cat carrier suspiciously. "Then why is he here?"

Lifting the carrier, Master Anderson smiled at the cat inside. "Ghost likes to join me on my errands these days, so I figured I'd bring him here so he can hang with his old man while I visit you guys."

Sir raised an eyebrow in disbelief.

"What? Don't you trust me?"

"Four words. 'Mucking. Out. The. Stalls.'"

Master Anderson burst out in a full-on belly laugh. "Fair enough…"

Brie looked at both men, curious about the private joke. Sir had referenced it before and it always seemed to elicit the same humorous response from Master Anderson. Why cleaning out a horse stall was funny remained a mystery to her.

"You going to let me in or not?" Master Anderson demanded.

"Certainly. In fact, I have a cat box you might like to clean," Sir replied, stepping to the side.

Master Anderson slapped him on the back in passing. "Only if you join me, buddy."

Shadow was waiting for them, his tail twitching back and forth as he stared at the large carrier in Master Anderson's hand.

Setting it down on the floor, Master Anderson undid the latch and Ghost slowly made his way out. He sat on his haunches and the two black cats stared at each other from a distance.

"I wonder what they're thinking," Brie mused.

From the other side of the room, Hope let out a happy screech as she made a beeline toward the cats, crawling like it was an Olympian sport.

Unused to a rambunctious child, Ghost stiffened and looked as if he was about to dart back into the carrier for safety.

When Hope reached Shadow, she sat down beside him and stared at the two cats in wonder, clapping her hands together. "Dow...dow!"

Shadow rubbed his cheek against her before walking over to Ghost. Hope followed him and held out her grasping hand to the unfamiliar cat. Ghost looked up at Master Anderson before tentatively sniffing at her fingers.

"Looks like Ghost feels the same way about babies as I do," he chuckled.

Hope squealed with joy when the cat's whiskers brushed against her fingers. Ghost backed up a step, staring at her with wide eyes as she scooted in between the two cats.

To his credit, the cat didn't move when Hope began patting Shadow and then reached out her other hand to do the same to him.

The look of sheer bliss on Hope's face while she petted the two cats tickled Brie's heart. "I think our little girl is in heaven."

Sir stared down at Hope tenderly, telling Master Anderson, "Now that you have our daughter thoroughly entertained, do you mind telling me why you're here?"

Master Anderson snorted. "Can't a man come and spend time with his good friends without being judged?"

"As busy as you are at the Center right now, I would say no."

Master Anderson shook his head. "You are a cynical man, Thane Davis."

"I noticed you still haven't answered my question."

Master Anderson smirked, holding up his hands. "What can I say, you got me."

"What's this all about?" Brie asked, intrigued.

"Funny you should ask, young Brie…" he said with a twinkle in his eye. "Because it involves you."

"Spill it, Anderson," Sir snorted.

Throwing his arm around Sir's shoulder, he said, "You may not know this, but our mutual Russian friend not only broke into my house but pranked me with your little subbie's help."

Brie blushed, remembering that day.

Sir nodded. "I do remember her mentioning it to me, but that was quite a while back."

"It was," Master Anderson agreed. "But some things take time to perfect."

Sir chuckled. "I can't believe you and Durov still act like children after all these years."

Master Anderson bumped shoulders with him. "What can I say? It keeps us young, unlike you, who is headed at breakneck speed to wise old man status."

Sir growled under his breath.

Master Anderson backed away, laughing. "Just stating it like it is, buddy."

Brie looked at Master Anderson guiltily, confessing, "I do feel bad about breaking into your house."

He turned to her and grinned. "Admit it. You had fun hiding those whoopee cushions all over my house."

She blushed a deeper shade of red. "Maybe…"

"Really, Brie," Sir chided, but she noticed the slight curve of a smile that tugged at the corners of his lips.

"I have a confession of my own to make, actually," Master Anderson announced. "Even though I was the victim of your little prank, I've never laughed as hard as I did while finding those little fuckers all over my house. Hell, the last one was a month ago. It's like they keep breeding or something."

Brie giggled.

"What exactly do you have planned?" Sir asked. "Wait, I don't want to know."

"Look. It's really an act of charity. Durov has been in a rough spot for a while now, and I just want to lift his spirits with the perfect prank."

Sir looked at him questioningly. "Fine. What has this got to do with Brie?"

"Well, I thought it only fair that she helps me pay him back."

Sir pressed his lips together. "Durov did fail to ask permission when he utilized my sub in such a manner…"

Master Anderson nodded triumphantly.

"As far as I'm concerned, that makes him fair game," Sir concluded. He glanced at Brie, "But I don't want to know any of the details so I have plausible deniability."

"I promise, Sir." Brie grinned.

Master Anderson slapped Sir on the back. "I'm glad you see it my way."

Brie giggled, excited at the prospect of being part of another prank. "What do you need me to do?"

Master Anderson winked at her. "I'll tell you on the way out."

"What? You mean we're doing it now?"

"Of course. There's no time like the present, young Brie."

Turning to Sir, he said with a grin, "Talk about a gift to you. You get to sit back and relax while you watch your kiddo entertain herself with the cats."

Sir smirked. "Hmm...it seems you thought of everything."

His eyes flashed with excitement. "Oh, I have!"

Placing an arm around Brie's shoulders, he started walking her to the door. "This is going to be simple, really..."

He stopped for a moment and spoke to Ghost, who still seemed wary of Hope. "Don't forget to give your old man some crap while I'm gone. And, remember, you can always escape to the cat carrier if things get a bit much with the kid."

"Don't worry. I'll be watching them closely," Sir assured him.

Shadow broke away from Hope and walked up to Master Anderson. He stared at the Dom without blinking his eyes.

"I've never seen a cat so full of himself," he snorted.

Brie giggled. "Is it possible you're a little jealous of him because Cayenne loves Shadow more than you?"

Master Anderson looked at her in shock. "How dare you suggest such a thing, young Brie. Of course she loves me best."

Laughing harder, Brie told him, "Sorry to burst your bubble, Master Anderson, but that's the fate of protective fathers."

"I'll forget you ever said that." He grabbed her hand, heading toward the door. Taking her to his truck, Master Anderson opened the passenger door and handed her a box wrapped in brown paper. "Be careful with these."

He picked up a larger box for himself before shutting the door and walking toward Rytsar's home. "Damn, this is going to be fun!"

Master Anderson was famous for his pranks—his creativity and thoroughness in executing them were legendary. But, in all the years she'd know him, Brie had never seen him quite this excited.

"I heard that Durov is back in Russia for a stint and figured this was the best time to strike."

Looking at the box she carried, Brie asked, "What's in here?"

"I'll let you know in a minute." A crooked smile spread across his face as they strolled up to the porch. He placed his box down and took hers, setting it on top.

"Now, ring the doorbell."

Brie had no idea what she was getting herself into and held her breath as she pressed it. Little Sparrow started barking, but no one answered.

"No one seems to be home."

"That's what I wanted to verify. Could you type in the code to unlock the door, young Brie?"

Her heart raced. "You want me to break into his house?"

Master Anderson raised an eyebrow. "It's no different than when you two broke into my house, now is it? Turnabout is fair play, but this time there won't be any interruptions." He turned away from her. "Go ahead. I won't peek."

Brie felt wickedly naughty as she typed in the code

and heard the lock slide back. "I hope he can forgive me…"

"He'll be thanking you, often and profusely. Trust me."

He picked up the box wrapped in brown paper and smiled. "Now you can unwrap the box."

Brie ripped at the brown paper and then let out a gasp when she saw what it was.

Master Anderson's green eyes twinkled in mirth. "The only proper payback for the whoopee cushion incident, wouldn't you say?"

She put a hand to her mouth, giggling. "You are so *bad*, Master Anderson."

"I'm so good, you mean. That poor Russian had no idea what he unleashed when he pranked me in my own home."

She looked down at the box again. "How do they work?"

"What? You've never seen a fart bomb before?"

She laughed. "No, never."

"They're a ton of fun. Here, let me show you." He opened up the lip of the box and pulled out a foiled square that looked suspiciously like a condom except for the smiley face printed on it.

"All you do is squish the little tab inside until you feel it break, and then you throw it."

She watched as he put the silver square between his thumb and fingers and squeezed it. He then tossed the foil square away from them.

She stared at it, convinced he was pranking her when nothing happened.

"Just wait…" he assured her.

Brie watched as the foil packet slowly grew bigger

and bigger until it finally popped and she caught the whiff of an obnoxious odor.

"That smells terrible!"

He chuckled, handing her a package. "Here. You try it."

Entranced by the magical element of the toy, Brie happily pressed the smiley face, breaking the tab between her fingers, then quickly tossed it, not wanting it to explode anywhere near her.

She watched it slowly puff up, but after waiting several moments, nothing happened. "Huh, I think I got a dud…" She felt a pang of disappointment.

He smirked. "You must be patient, young grasshopper."

Sure enough, a few seconds later, Brie heard the satisfying pop, and the air filled with the unpleasant scent.

"Whoopee cushions have nothing on these babies!" Master Anderson grinned like a little kid.

Brie looked down at the box again, shaking her head in disbelief. "It says there are seventy-two in here. Are we going to hide them all?"

"Naturally—minus the two we just used." He snagged another one and slipped it into his pocket, winking at her. "For good luck."

When Master Anderson opened the door, Little Sparrow barked at him but immediately quieted down when Brie walked through the door.

"It's all right, girl," Brie cooed, kneeling to pet her.

Little Sparrow rushed to her, so happy to see Brie that the dog wagged her entire body and not just her tail.

"I wonder who is taking care of her?"

"A friend of mine. Durov reached out to me and asked if I knew someone nearby who could watch her while he was out." Master Anderson snorted. "Little did he know he was giving me the perfect opportunity to pay him back."

Master Anderson set his box down and nodded at Little Sparrow. "This pup reminds me of Kiah, one of my favorite companions when I was younger." He reached into the box and pulled out a leash, along with a large meaty bone wrapped in plastic. "While we hide the evidence, she'll be happily munching on the bone outside."

"You've thought of everything," Brie stated, truly impressed.

Little Sparrow stared at the bone in his hand, licking her lips excitedly. Master Anderson clicked the leash to her collar and led her outside.

Brie watched through the large windows as he secured Little Sparrow and then, with a stylish flourish, unwrapped the bone for her.

The dog jumped up and down excitedly when he presented it to her. Taking the large bone in her mouth, she lay down and began gnawing on it contentedly.

Master Anderson returned and washed his hands, smiling as he watched Little Sparrow enjoying her treat.

Brie loved that about the sexy Dom. His love for animals was part of his charm.

After drying his hands, he walked to her and took one of the silver packets out of the box, stating solemnly, "You get the honor of placing the first one, young Brie."

"Thank you, Master Anderson."

"You'll need to place it where it will get enough pressure to break the tab or it won't work."

"Understood."

Brie took the packet from him and looked around

the room. Walking to the couch, she slipped it under the cushion, strategically placing it on the frame of the furniture so it would receive enough pressure when someone sat down. She then carefully repositioned the seat cushion and smiled at him.

Master Anderson nodded his approval. "Well done."

"What else do you have in that big box you brought?" she asked, looking over at it.

"I've created little booby traps, so to speak," he stated with pride. "While you place these in unusual places around the house, I will be setting them up in more obvious places. The only catch is he won't be able to prevent the bomb from exploding once he triggers it. Would you like to see what I mean?"

"Please!"

Master Anderson took a small contraption out of the box and walked to the kitchen cupboards. He searched through them until he found the jars of pickles. "Since we know Durov loves these with his vodka, it seems only appropriate to christen them with this gift." He placed the contraption inside the cupboard next to the jars of pickles.

"Toss me one of those babies."

Brie fished out a foil packet but didn't trust herself to throw it to him without mishap, so she walked it over to him instead.

Master Anderson placed the packet into his contraption and carefully set it before closing the cabinet door. He grinned at Brie. "I suspect Durov will have activated a couple by the time he goes for the pickles. When he opens the cabinet door, the bomb will be activated, and he'll know it's about to blow—that's when the fun begins!"

Brie could just imagine Rytsar sprinting to the door with the bomb in his hand, hoping to make it outside in time.

"You really are an evil genius."

Master Anderson tipped an imaginary hat at her. "I wear the name proudly."

Brie looked down at all of the smiling packets and shook her head. "You do realize you're going to have an irate Russian on your hands."

He smirked, shrugging. "I'm not worried. When he threw down the gauntlet, he knew there would be consequences."

Because Master Anderson had never reacted to the whoopee cushion prank Rytsar had pulled on him with Brie's help, Rytsar wouldn't see this coming. Although there was a chance he might never forgive her, Brie was enjoying this practical joke a little too much.

"I'll start placing my contraptions while you figure out where you are hiding yours." Master Anderson grabbed a large handful of the foil packets and tossed them in his box.

Feeling inspired, she walked to the barstools lining the kitchen counter and lifted the front leg of one, slipping the foil pouch underneath it and gently setting it down.

"Nice," he praised her while booby-trapping the trash can.

"Poor Rytsar," she giggled.

"Think of every fart bomb as an expression of our admiration."

Brie laughed as she headed to Rytsar's bedroom. She walked into his closet and looked at his row of shoes. Placing them in the toe of the shoe would hide it but it wouldn't provide the pressure necessary, so she chose his leather boots in the back. Brie slipped it inside the heel of his boot and carefully set it back in place. With luck, months from now, Rytsar would slip it on without thinking and the pressure of his heel would end up breaking the tab before he could prevent it.

Satisfied, Brie wandered into his bathroom. Spying the toilet, she burst into giggles. Although it was obvious and had no chance of tricking him, Brie lifted the lid and placed a silver packet smiley side up on the lip of the bowl where the bumper from the toilet seat would make contact. She gingerly put the seat down and stepped away.

The fact that it was a fart bomb made this placement the funniest yet. Brie figured Rytsar would see the humor in it when he lifted the lid to pee.

Moving out of his room, Brie headed down the hallway and caught Master Anderson staring at the bedroom Rytsar had designed for Hope. Turning to her, he said, "As tempting as it is, there are some lines that must not be crossed." Then he grinned, "However, he will go crazy assuming that I've crossed them."

Master Anderson chuckled as he moved on to the laundry room instead.

As much as he hated babies himself, Brie appreciated that he respected Rytsar's love for Hope.

Just like the whoopee cushion adventure, Brie had fun while she walked around Rytsar's home, placing the silver packets in places she hoped would surprise him.

Hours later, when they were finally done hiding all sixty-nine of the bombs, Master Anderson let out a satisfied sigh. "I can't tell you the feeling of accomplishment I am experiencing right now, young Brie. Durov is in for some fun times ahead."

She laughed. "I doubt he will see it that way."

"I wholeheartedly disagree. He'll appreciate the time and effort that went into this gift and be humbled by it."

Brie snorted with amusement.

After bringing Little Sparrow back in and double-checking to make sure everything looked the way Rytsar had left it, Master Anderson commanded Brie to lock the door behind them.

He chuckled, grinning like the Cheshire Cat as he escorted her back to their house. Once inside, he announced, "Thane, old buddy, it's time to celebrate!"

Sir stood up from the couch as he turned to greet them. "Well, that certainly took a while."

"You can't rush perfection…" Master Anderson's jaw suddenly dropped and he muttered, *"Et tu, Brute?"*

Brie glanced in the direction he was looking and saw Ghost laid out on his back with his eyes closed, purring loudly as Hope cuddled between the two cats.

"The three of them have been like that for hours," Sir told him.

Master Anderson shook his head in shock. "I can't believe Ghost went soft like that. I thought he and I were kindred spirits."

Brie bumped against him. "Maybe you are. I think you should spend an afternoon with Hope and find out what you're missing."

"Hmm…"

She smiled at him in surprise. "What? Are you considering it?"

Master Anderson stared at Hope, then nodded his head slowly as if he were seriously contemplating it. "I'm not the kind of man to shirk from a challenge. I suppose it could prove interesting…"

"Our daughter is not to be used as an experiment," Sir grumbled.

Master Anderson chuckled. "Of course not, I'm just saying… If you ever have a need, I'd be willing to watch her. One time. But not overnight." He shuddered. "No way could I handle a whole night."

"We'll keep you in mind," Sir said in a sarcastic tone.

"Anyway…" Master Anderson muttered, changing the subject. "It's time to celebrate." He walked into their kitchen and got out three glasses and a bottle of whiskey. "Do you want your whiskey neat or on the rocks, young Brie?"

"Neither."

Master Anderson frowned slightly. "Okay…"

Turning to Sir, he asked, "What about you, buddy?"

"I'm afraid I must abstain, as well."

Master Anderson's face suddenly fell. "No…"

He looked at Brie. "Say it ain't so."

She giggled, rubbing her stomach tenderly. "It's true."

He looked back at Sir, shaking his head. "Can't you let the poor girl have a breather? Back to back babies are a bit much."

Sir smiled, enjoying his reaction. "I'm afraid when you get to be our age, it becomes a necessity."

Master Anderson got a troubled look on his face. "Hadn't considered that…"

"I don't want to raise toddlers when I'm forty," Sir added.

"Wise. I can't think of anything worse."

Master Anderson's face suddenly lit up. Wagging his finger at her, he said with admiration, "Oh, you're a crafty one. You got me good there. Had me hook, line, and sinker. Well played, young lady."

"I wish I could take credit." Brie walked to the refrigerator, pulled out the carton of coconut water, and set it next to the glasses. "But we aren't joking."

Master Anderson stared down at the carton with a look of resignation. "Well...I guess there is nothing to be done then." He poured two glasses of coconut water and handed one to each of them.

Taking his glass of whiskey, he raised it. "Here's to one of the best pranks played in human history...and to another little snot-nosed kid in the family. Cheers!"

Sir winked at Brie, a look of amusement on his face.

Brie smiled at Sir and held up her tumbler, clinking glasses with both men, savoring the sweet taste of the coconut water.

She glanced at the cats lying so contentedly next to Hope. Brie had no doubt that despite all Master Anderson's posturing and his insistence that he disliked children, deep down he was a big softy.

She was confident it wouldn't take long before he caved just like Ghost, and grinned at the sexy Dom as she took another sip.

Just you wait, Master Anderson...

The Rose

"Are you Mrs. Brianna Davis?"

"I am." Brie stared in wonder at the massive bouquet of long-stemmed roses.

"Then these are for you."

She blushed as she took the large vase of red roses from the delivery person. It was so huge she could barely hold the vase with both hands.

"Wait and I'll get you a tip."

"No need, ma'am. Already taken care of."

She thanked him from behind the large bouquet as he shut the door for her.

Laughing, she walked into the great room and set the vase on the coffee table. Stepping back, she stared in pleasant bewilderment at the extravagant bouquet.

Curious why Sir had sent it, Brie looked for a card but found none.

Since he was in downtown LA at a business meeting, she immediately texted him.

I just received an incredible bouquet that must be from you. What's the occasion?

A few moments later, he texted back two simple

words.

My secret.

As she looked back at the bouquet, Brie put her hands to her heart, overcome with immense joy and love for her Master. Despite all the difficulties they were facing, this romantic gesture reminded her of how incredibly lucky she was.

She reached out and took one of the large blossoms in her hand, leaning in to enjoy its scent.

This is what love smells like, she thought to herself.

Brie picked up the huge vase and carried it upstairs to her office so she could enjoy it while she worked.

She heard Hope babbling to herself from the nursery soon after waking from her nap.

Carrying Hope into her office, Brie laid a blanket on the floor and set her on it, tossing Hope's favorite toys around her. Naturally, Shadow soon joined the baby on the blanket.

Brie looked at the bouquet again with profound gratitude.

Holloway was still threatening her career—the horrible man remained hell-bent on personally seeing that her second film was never produced. However, there was something positive coming from it. This unexpected break allowed Brie to bask in the joy of being a mom while she planned out her *next* film project.

Listening to the sound of Hope's playful giggles, Brie turned on her computer and opened the photos she had taken of Gino Mancini's black book. Although she felt slightly guilty, knowing he didn't want her recording materials from his collection, she felt justified using them because she hadn't known at the time she'd taken the pictures.

Besides, the pages were simply a list of the dates and places of every event Alonzo Davis had performed at when he was alive.

There was nothing personal or proprietary in Gino's black book. But having that list was invaluable to Brie because it allowed her to easily surf the web to find additional information about Alonzo's professional life as a violinist.

Brie was so completely lost in her research that she was startled when Sir walked up behind her. "Enjoying yourself?"

She spun around in her chair. "Back so soon?"

He looked at his watch. "It's five o'clock."

She giggled, glancing at Hope. "I've been having such fun, I guess I lost all sense of time."

He smiled at her with tenderness. "I'm glad to hear it."

Getting up from her chair, she rushed into his embrace. "I'm even happier, now that you're here." She sighed in contentment when he kissed the top of her head.

"I see you brought the flowers up here."

Brie glanced at them and smiled. "It is the most magnificent bouquet I have ever seen."

Sir squeezed her tighter. "I have plans for it tonight."

She looked up at him questioningly.

In answer, he grasped the back of her neck and gave her a passionate kiss that left her utterly breathless. "I want to spend a quiet evening with you—just the two of us."

"What about Hope?"

"Not to worry. That's already been arranged."

She smiled up at him. "Are your aunt and uncle coming to get her?"

He shook his head.

"Who, then?"

"It's a surprise," he answered with a glint in his eye as he picked Hope up and started toward the stairs.

She giggled, then looked back at the bouquet to admire it. Sir certainly took pleasure in surprising her—in and out of the bedroom.

As they headed downstairs together, he commanded, "I want you to dress up for me. Pick your favorite gown, the one that makes you smile when you put it on."

"It's going to be hard to decide," she confessed. "There's so many, Sir."

He raised an eyebrow, stating in a low, seductive voice, "Then I look forward to seeing which one you choose."

When Sir swatted her on the ass, she let out an excited squeak as she turned from him to head to the bedroom.

Brie felt butterflies start as she walked into the room and opened the closet doors. Although she had many beautiful dresses, there was one that remained her favorite.

She pulled it from the hanger, smiling as she walked out and placed it on the bed. Inspired, Brie turned on a playlist of Italian songs while she got ready for him.

Stripping out of her clothes, Brie picked up the dress and slipped it on, purring as the thin, silken material caressed her skin and slid down into place. What she loved even more about this particular dress was the way it swayed when she walked—so sexy and alluring.

Brie walked into the bathroom to look in the mirror. She was still as enchanted by the dress as she had been the day Sir gave it to her.

The simple white dress with a flared skirt had a modest style that was incredibly sexy because she wore nothing underneath it—just as she had that night in Venice. The dress had an air of innocence. However, the enticing way her nipples protruded from under the thin material was deliciously tantalizing to Sir.

She slowly brushed out her hair, remembering when she had danced with Sir in the flooded piazza of San Marco while wearing this dress. She'd never forgotten the way he had guided her through the shallow water in a slow waltz before an audience of bystanders. It was a unique and romantic moment she cherished.

Looking at herself in the mirror, Brie suddenly realized she had forgotten one important element. Searching through her drawers, she finally found the length of white lace. Using it as a headband to hold her hair away from her face, Brie teased her long curls until she was satisfied that she looked the same as she had that night in Venice.

To finish off the look, Brie applied light makeup to enhance her eyes and added just a blush of pink to her lips. Pouting seductively, she twirled in front of the mirror delighting in the feel of the dress as it moved.

Rather than completing the outfit with shoes, Brie chose to go barefoot in remembrance of their dance. Feeling utterly irresistible, she turned off the music and walked out of the bedroom, intent on seducing Sir.

"Well, hello."

Brie stopped dead in her tracks when she saw Master Anderson standing there, holding Hope's diaper bag.

Down the hallway, she heard Sir listing off instructions. "She'll need to go down at eight. It's totally normal for her to fuss a little. If you have any questions, I have everything written down in the instruct—"

The moment Sir walked into the room and saw Brie, he forgot what he was saying and stood there, staring at her.

"Babygirl…"

The look of desire in his gaze made her blush.

In a voice mixed with admiration and lust, he stated, "I stand in awe of you."

Master Anderson cleared his throat beside her.

Brie looked in his direction, having completely forgotten he was there.

"Yes, that there is a mighty fine dress…" Master Anderson said gruffly. Turning to face Sir, he stammered, "I, ah…yeah…so, kid goes down at what time again?"

"Eight," Sir replied, handing Hope over to him. "All your questions are answered in the instructions I gave you." He put his hand on Master Anderson's shoulder as he walked him toward the door. "If at any point you want to cry 'uncle' feel free to call my uncle and he'll swing by to pick her up."

Master Anderson chuckled. "I see what you did there. You want me to literally call an uncle if I can't handle it. Very funny."

Sir patted his back. "I have faith in you."

"Sure you do."

"Let me help you get her into the car seat…"

Brie watched the two men leave. She couldn't believe that Sir had taken Master Anderson up on his offer to babysit, or that the cowboy had actually agreed to it.

Knowing the Reynolds were ready to act as his backup was reassuring for her, because she couldn't begin to imagine how the next few hours were going to play out for him.

Hopefully, Shey would be there to act as moral support and help him get through the evening without incident.

Sir returned several minutes later and locked the front door.

"Now, where were we?"

Brie twisted where she stood, looking at him in anticipation.

Her Master stared at her hungrily, shaking his head in disbelief. "Looking at you tonight, it's as if no time has passed since you first wore that dress."

She bowed her head, gratified to hear it. "I love everything about this dress, Sir."

Sir held his finger up for silence and then left to turn on the music. Soon, the sweet, haunting melody of his father's violin filled the air.

He returned to her and held out his hand. "Shall we dance, wife?"

"Please, husband."

Sir grasped her hand firmly, resting his other in the small of her back. Brie glided across the floor in his strong arms, reliving that dance on the piazza.

Unlike the first time, however, Sir let his hands wander as they moved together, lightly brushing against her nipples and cupping her ass as they danced.

"I can't resist you," he growled in a husky voice, sweeping her off her feet before the song was even finished. Carrying her into the bedroom, he stopped to kiss her before setting her down.

Brie parted her lips as she responded to his desire, moaning softly when he claimed her with his tongue.

The kiss left her so lightheaded afterward, she stumbled weakly when her feet touched the floor.

"Are you okay?" he asked with amusement.

"Your kisses slay me, Sir."

He grazed her lips with his finger. "Tonight, we use our given names."

Brie nodded, the butterflies starting up again. She wondered the reason for his change in protocol.

He pointed to the vase. "I brought these down because I want you to choose one."

Brie felt a surge of excitement as she approached the massive bouquet. Now she knew the true purpose for the flowers.

"Pick the most exquisite rose from the arrangement," he instructed.

Brie nodded and walked around the bouquet as she looked over each flower carefully. When she had narrowed it down, she pulled the winning rose from the vase. The bloom was huge, every petal perfectly formed. As a final test, Brie breathed in its intoxicating scent and purred in pleasure.

Sir moved up behind her and lightly grazed her cheek with the back of his hand as he whispered in a low, husky voice, "Brianna…"

Erotic chills coursed through her and she wondered if he knew the power his voice had over her body.

"Are you confident in your choice?" he asked, nuzzling her neck.

She breathed in its heavenly scent again. "I am. This rose is truly exquisite in every way."

He gazed down at the flower. "Good. I want only the best for my goddess."

Brie closed her eyes as Sir slowly ran his hand down

her arm, causing goosebumps to rise on her skin.

"Do you remember the first time we scened with a rose?"

"I do," Brie answered breathlessly. "It was at the Training Center..." She paused for a moment, purring softly. "You used the petals to cover my eyes."

"I did," he replied in a gruff voice, lightly tracing the line of her collar-bone.

Brie had never forgotten that night. He'd begun the lesson by informing her that the human brain was capable of taking a simple stimulus and magnifying it many times greater than it was, then he had used that power to magnify his simple caress into an orgasmic experience.

She suspected it was the reason he preferred using his touch over traditional BDSM tools. Truthfully, *any* lesson from him was guaranteed to be incredibly erotic and satisfying.

"Tonight, I have a new lesson for you."

Brie gripped the stem of the rose tighter, completely enchanted at the idea of another lesson with a rose under the skillful hands of her Master.

"You will focus all of your senses on me while I make slow, passionate love to you, Brie."

She glanced down at the rose, trembling in anticipation.

Sir was no ordinary man. Many Doms only played out their own fantasies with their subs, sacrificing the intimate act of lovemaking in exchange for fulfilling their physical desires.

However, Sir did not accept such limitations. He encouraged the emotional side of their connection and could be as equally tender and loving as he could be rough and demanding.

The love she felt for him at that moment was so intense it almost hurt.

Brie held her breath as he lightly grazed her jawline with his fingertips. Her skin tingled wherever he touched her.

Sir's caress was so tender and reverent it made tears well up in her eyes. There was no doubt that this man's feelings for her were equally intense.

"I love you, Thane," she whispered.

He responded to her declaration by tilting her head to the side to expose her neck and growling. "Be still and do not drop the rose."

Her heart skipped a beat when his warm lips landed on her throat. When she felt the pressure of his teeth against her skin, it sent currents of sensual electricity through her and she moaned in response.

Sir slipped off the material of her dress to expose her shoulder, leaving trails of kisses and light bites.

Brie trembled, feeling deliciously weak from his sensual attention.

"I enjoy seeing you in this dress. However, I love seeing you out of it even more." Carefully lifting the dress over her head so she would not lose her grip on the rose, he let it drop to the floor beside them.

"Ah, yes..." he murmured, running his hands over her naked skin.

He gave her a ravenous smile as he turned her around, looking over every inch of her body. "Perfection."

Brie cherished his praise, feeling fully and wholly beautiful in his eyes.

"I long to feel your naked skin against mine," he

stated with a sultry smile as he slowly undressed before her.

She stared at him, entranced by his masculine body. From his toned chest and hard shaft to his tight ass that flexed as he moved, the man was majestic naked.

Sir returned to her, wrapping his arms around her from behind. Still clutching the rose, she leaned back against his chest, aroused by his scent—it was a combination of musk mixed with a hint of sweetness that reminded her of a summer's day.

"Much better," he growled, pressing his hard cock against her as he grazed her nipples with his hands, causing them to contract into tight buds.

The chemistry between them was so powerful, her body ached with need.

"I love everything about you, Thane," she purred softly. Her heart thrilled every time she said his name.

"The feeling is mutual," he told her lustfully.

Gripping the rose with both hands had a similar effect to being handcuffed. It gave her a feeling of vulnerability which she thoroughly enjoyed.

Brie bit her lip when he began lightly rolling her nipple between his fingers. The erotic stimulation instantly made her pussy wet.

"Do you know what I want, Brie?"

Her heart quickened. "Tell me."

"To watch my cock disappear down your throat."

Brie smiled up at him as he helped her to her knees while she still held the flower. The blossom rested between her breasts. It was a powerful pose Brie enjoyed and he had made it unique with the addition of the rose.

"Open that pretty little mouth."

Brie parted her lips for him and moaned when he

fisted her hair and guided his cock into her mouth. Sir was gentle and slow, making love to her throat like he would her pussy. The fragrant scent of the rose added to the familiar action of sucking his cock, enhancing the experience.

Brie looked up at him in adoration as she deepthroated him.

"I like it when you focus on my cock," he murmured gruffly.

She moaned in agreement, completely at his mercy as he guided her movements. But the stimulation proved too much, and he had to pull out.

"Not yet…"

Helping Brie back to her feet, he led her to their tantra chair. "Lie down and let your husband play with you."

Brie straddled the leather chaise lounge, still clutching the rose in her hands as she slid down into the comfortable curvature of it. The position left her legs spread wide for him.

Sir knelt beside her and began kissing her on the lips while his fingers sought out her wet pussy.

Instead of playing with her clit, he surprised her by lightly slapping her pussy with the palm of his hand. It was such an unexpected and possessive act that her pussy quivered. Each slap caused erotic jolts to reverberate through her, driving her to distraction.

Brie moaned, lost in the sensual spell he weaved with his passionate kisses and the magic of his masculine touch.

Knowing her body well, it did not take long for him to encourage the first telltale signs of her mounting orgasm.

She whimpered, pressing her pussy against his hand.

Knowing she was close, he commanded, "Come while I kiss you, Brie."

She groaned in anticipation, eager for the intimacy of climaxing for him while he claimed her mouth. When the orgasm hit, it was quick and strong, leaving her breathless afterward.

"Again," he stated hungrily.

Brie willingly gave in to his desire, not fighting the delicious feelings when she felt another orgasm building in intensity. Concentrating on his ardent kisses and the intoxicating scent of the rose, she surrendered completely to it.

The moment the second climax washed over her, she tensed, overwhelmed by the power of it.

"It seems you are desperate for release," he growled afterward.

She blushed. "I guess my body is greedy for you."

He chuckled. "Shall we see if you can come with just a kiss?"

She nodded, certain she could.

Brie closed her eyes, submitting to his demanding kiss as he explored her mouth with his tongue. Her body was primed for another climax, but she rode the intense crest of it for a few moments before surrendering to it.

Afterward, she stared at him in a state of awe. The man played her body like an instrument, knowing exactly which strings to pluck.

Sir smiled at her in satisfaction. "I love watching you come, but I enjoy feeling it even more."

Leaning down, he began sucking on her nipple as he slipped a finger inside her and began stroking her G-spot. The spell he had her under made it impossible for her not to come immediately.

Within seconds, her body started tensing in preparation for the next orgasm. Sir groaned his approval as her pussy began pulsing around his finger.

"Good girl…"

Brie was in such an aroused state, she was completely at his mercy.

"Now, let's change your position," he stated. Helping her to her feet, he had Brie lean her torso against the higher curve of the tantra chair so her ass was exposed to him.

Smiling ravenously, he commanded, "Hold the rose directly in front of you. Do not drop it under any circumstances."

Sir spanked her ass, causing pleasant tingles to course through her body. He then slid his cock into her pussy while his fingers played with her tight rosette. Brie moaned loudly, enjoying the dual stimulation.

"Are you going to come for me again, Brie?"

"Yes," she purred in excitement.

He began ramming his shaft into her repeatedly, each stroke teasing her swollen G-spot while he slowly pressed his thumb into her ass.

Her orgasm climbed to dizzying heights. When her thighs began to tremble, she struggled to keep holding the rose.

Brie cried out when she climaxed, her pussy gushing as she released, covering the tantra chair in her come.

Sir let out a guttural growl when he felt her slick excitement.

She lay against the tantra chair, her body still trembling from her multiple orgasms, and held on to the rose for dear life.

"I think the time has come," he murmured huskily as he bit her shoulder, "for me to unleash my love on you."

"Yes, Thane," she begged.

Fisting her hair, he pulled her head back. "Keep your eyes on the rose until you can no longer focus. I'm about to make you fly."

Brie held her breath when Sir let go of her hair and grabbed her waist with both hands. He ramped up the strength and speed of his thrusts. She was far too stimulated not to respond to the ferocity of his claiming.

With his permission, Brie willingly dove into that sweet abyss of subspace and eventually dropped the rose.

Although she was partially aware of her surroundings, she was flying so high afterward that she was unable to respond when he picked her up and carried her to the bed.

"Brie...focus on my voice."

She lay there, keeping her eyes open with great effort. Still floating on clouds of sensual bliss, she turned her head toward him as a slow smile spread across her lips.

"I love you, Thane Davis."

He grazed her bottom lip with the rose, declaring with a possessive look in his eyes, "There will never be another person who will love you as much as I do, Brie."

Heated Exchange

Master Anderson returned with Hope at exactly ten o'clock that same evening. Shey was standing by his side.

The sexy Dom looked a little worse for wear, but Hope seemed to be sleeping peacefully in the car seat he carried. "Here she is, safe and sound," he announced, holding her out to Sir.

"How did it go?" Brie asked, taking a quick peek at Hope.

"Like I said—she's safe and sound."

"So, no issues?" Sir confirmed.

Master Anderson took off his cowboy hat and swiped his hair back, chuckling. "Let's just say that little girl is a ball of energy. Even the cats are wiped out."

"Tell us all about it," Brie encouraged, inviting them both inside.

Master Anderson escorted Shey into the house, then headed straight for the couch. He flopped down on it, laying his head back and putting his hat over his eyes before sighing in exhaustion.

Sir smirked. "Did our daughter prove to be too

much for you?" he asked as he unbuckled Hope from the car seat and cradled her against him.

"I'm still standing, figuratively speaking," Master Anderson answered, pushing his hat up.

"Oh yes. Brad had it handled the entire time," Shey replied, laughing. "I was impressed by his mad skills."

"Don't be throwing your man under the bus, now," he teased.

"I would never do that," she assured him, then turned to Brie. "I even took pictures."

Brie giggled. "I would love to see them."

Shey fished her cell phone out of her purse. "Brad insisted on doing everything himself."

Brie glanced at Master Anderson, who shrugged at her. "I wasn't about to shirk on a challenge, although I was tempted a few times. Trust me."

Shey chuckled as she showed Brie her phone. "This was his first attempt at trying to change her diaper."

Master Anderson suddenly looked sick and covered his face with his hat again, muttering, "Don't remind me."

"As you can see by the expression on his face, it wasn't going well."

Brie burst out laughing when she saw the look of horror plastered on his face in the picture.

"But, Brad insisted on finishing the job," Shey continued proudly, swiping to the next picture.

Brie shook her head in amusement as she stared at the photo of Master Anderson donning a leather BDSM mask that covered his nose, along with rubber gloves and an apron. "I'm surprised Hope didn't freak out when she saw you in this getup."

"Oh, Brad cooed and sang sweet words to her while

he gagged as he changed her diaper." Shey turned to Master Anderson, smiling. "You really were adorable."

Master Anderson groaned. "Please, Shey. I'd rather not relive the moment, thank you."

"You would think a man used to mucking out horse stalls wouldn't even be fazed by it," Sir stated with an amused expression.

"Don't even go there, buddy. Horse manure smells like freaking flowers compared to what I experienced tonight."

"I'm glad Hope's asleep and can't hear what you're saying," Brie chided him.

"I mean no disrespect to your little girl, young Brie." He put his hand to his heart. "I'm just telling it like it is."

Shey held out her phone to show Brie another picture. "Here's Hope in the cat sanctuary. Talk about a kid in the candy store."

Brie laughed. "I bet."

"At first, the kittens didn't know what to make of her," Master Anderson told Brie.

He then turned to Sir. "That baby of yours is a crawling hellion. I have never seen a kid move that fast on all fours."

Brie smiled. "Shadow's been an excellent teacher."

Master Anderson sighed. "Well, lucky for me, my cats entertained her most of the night. All I had to do was sit back and enjoy the show."

"It was so precious, Brie," Shey told her. "It's like Hope and the kittens were all playing a complicated version of tag that only they understood. Every one of the cats got involved, and Hope was eating up all of the attention."

Brie noticed Hope's big smile in every one of the

pictures as Shey swiped through them. "She looks so happy!"

"I kind of hated to break them up when it was time to feed her," Master Anderson admitted.

Brie glanced at him, grinning. "And how did that go?"

"Naturally, I wasn't going to feed her that baby jar crap I found in the bag."

Sir raised an eyebrow. "What did you feed her, then?"

"A gourmet meal fit for royalty," he stated proudly.

"Brad spent an hour in the kitchen making it," Shey told them, smiling at Master Anderson tenderly.

Brie was impressed to hear it but was curious. "How did Hope like the meal?"

"She loved my cooking, of course. What baby wouldn't?" He then turned to Sir and said accusingly, "The instructions I was given didn't say anything about how to keep your kid still without a highchair, so...I had to improvise."

Shey bumped Brie's shoulder. "You're going to love these pictures."

Brie laughed when she saw the photo and walked over to Sir to show him. The picture showed Master Anderson in the kitchen, shirtless—which certainly wasn't a surprise—but he'd used his undershirt like a baby restraint to secure Hope to a chair.

"Ingenious," Sir praised him.

"That's what I thought," Master Anderson agreed. "Needless to say, the t-shirt was ruined."

He turned to Brie. "Your kid sure is a messy eater."

"She isn't even one yet," she reminded him, laughing.

"Anyway, feeding time was a huge success, so it was

worth the sacrifice."

"Bravo, Master Anderson!" Brie was truly impressed by his resourcefulness.

"It was smooth sailing after that." He swept his hand through his hair. "I just set the kid down with the cats and the rest is history."

He nodded to Shey. "Go ahead. Show them."

Shey dutifully showed her a picture of Hope sprawled out, asleep on the floor with Cayenne curled up against her. All the other cats sat around her in a circle.

"Cutest damn thing I've ever seen," Master Anderson stated. "Cayenne wouldn't leave her side the entire time."

Brie studied the adorable photo and smiled. "Cayenne probably smelled Shadow on her."

Master Anderson threw his hands up. "Now, why did you have to spoil that perfectly sweet picture for me? I'll never be able to look at it the same way again."

Brie chuckled. "Someday, you're going to admit that Shadow is one of the best things to ever happen to you and Cayenne."

He shook his head slowly. "Never going to happen."

Sir walked over to the couch with Hope in his arms and held out his hand to Master Anderson. "I didn't think you had it in you, but you proved me wrong tonight."

Master Anderson stood up and looked at him smugly. "Well, thank you, Thane. It's good to see you eat humble pie for once."

Sir glanced at Shey. "It must be a relief to know that under all of that bravado, he really could make a good father."

Master Anderson snorted. "That's not it at all. I just

proved I'm man enough for any challenge, no matter how difficult or disgusting."

He glanced at Brie, putting his hat against his chest. "Not that your child is disgusting, of course."

Brie laughed.

Shey agreed with Sir. "This experience tonight has really opened my eyes, Mr. Davis."

Master Anderson looked at Shey warily. "Now, don't be getting any ideas, darlin'. This was just a one-time thing. That's it."

Shey wrapped her arms around him. "I know, you big softie."

Master Anderson shot Sir a worried glance.

Sir smiled knowingly while he repositioned Hope higher on his shoulder. "I'd better get this little angel to bed. Brie, would you see our friends out?"

"Of course, Sir."

Brie had to hide her smile as she escorted them to the door and thanked Master Anderson again for babysitting.

After shutting the door behind them, she shook her head in astonishment.

Sir certainly is a devious one…

Brie was relieved to hear from Rytsar early the next day when he called to update them on the Lilly situation. They put him on speakerphone to hear what he had to share.

The first question that tumbled out of Brie's mouth was, "Are you okay?"

"I knew you would worry despite my best efforts, *radost moya.*" Rytsar chuckled. "*Da*, I am fine."

She breathed an audible sigh of relief, which made him chuckle even more.

"How did Lilly seem?" Sir asked.

Rytsar paused for a moment. "That is a complicated answer, *moy droog*. The woman is physically healthy, but as far as her mental state…"

"What?" he pressed.

"She has changed."

"In a good way, I hope," Brie said expectantly.

"Not exactly."

Sir growled. "What do you mean?"

"You will be gratified to know she is no longer in love with you, comrade. In fact, she loathes you."

Sir snorted. "Well, that's a relief."

"*Da.*"

"What's the problem, then?" Brie asked.

"The creature has a new interest."

Brie's heart dropped. "Who?"

Rytsar coughed uncomfortably. "She has developed an attraction to the Reverend Mother."

"Oh, my goodness!" Brie looked at Sir in shock.

"It has made it…umm…uncomfortable for the venerable woman."

"I can only imagine," Sir muttered. "What did Lilly say about her?"

"It's not what she said. It's what she's done."

"Oh, God…" Brie whimpered.

Rytsar snorted. "Do you really want to know, *radost moya?*"

"Of course."

"Very well…the creature has been caught spying on

the Reverend Mother and masturbating."

Sir groaned. "Does her depravity know no depths?"

"Dr. Volkov believes it is a form of Stockholm Syndrome. Because the Reverend Mother runs the convent where she is being held and oversees her care, the creature has bonded with her."

"Is this the reason the Reverend Mother is stepping down from her position?"

"I believe so, although she refuses to admit it. She tells me that she believes the creature is no longer progressing, and she blames herself for the failure."

"She is not at fault," Sir stated with disgust.

"I agree, comrade. However, I have not been able to convince the Reverend Mother of that."

"What did Dr. Volkov have to say?" Brie asked.

"After a thorough psychological examination, he's concluded that the creature suffers from a delusional disorder and will continue to need twenty-four-seven care during treatment."

"So, he believes she can be treated?" Sir asked, stunned.

Rytsar hesitated when he answered. "He believes with proper medical treatment and psychotherapy, she may recover. However, her delusional disorder is highly resistant to medication alone. People with severe symptoms must be hospitalized to prevent them from hurting others until the condition can be stabilized."

"Does he have any idea how long that will take?"

"No, *moy droog*. He told me he has never encountered a case as severe as hers."

Goosebumps rose on Brie's skin. To hear from a medical doctor that Lilly was mentally psychotic and a danger to others cemented her greatest fears.

Sir growled. "I don't like this. No hospital is secure enough to hold her."

"I agree," Brie cried. "Lilly would escape at the first opportunity."

"I concur," Rytsar stated.

"But you did say she is no longer obsessed with Sir. That is a positive step, right?" Brie asked, needing something to hold onto.

"Not necessarily," Rytsar answered.

Sir furrowed his brow. "Why is that?"

"She wants to make you pay for abandoning her child."

"God, will this insanity ever end?" he snarled.

"It could," Rytsar replied. "Just say the word."

Brie's heart began to race. She understood his offer. It was frightening to know that with one word, they could end Lilly's life and move on as if it never happened. It would be so simple and yet so monstrous.

She stared at the phone after the call ended. She had hoped for better news and was struggling with what they had just learned.

Sir broke the unnerving silence. "Excuse me. I need to make a phone call."

He left the room abruptly, heading into his office.

Brie looked at Hope, innocently playing in her bouncer. Whatever decision they made would ultimately boil down to keeping Hope and their new child safe. The question was—would they be able to live with it?

When Sir came out of his office an hour later, he informed her, "The meeting you and I discussed was set for Friday, but I've rescheduled it for tonight. Can you be ready by seven?"

"Absolutely, Sir."

"Good." He looked down at the floor with a pained expression.

Brie understood he was anxious about confronting his past with Lilly, but she knew it was vital he face it now after hearing the recent news.

Smiling at him encouragingly, she asked, "Should I call the Reynolds to pick up Hope?"

"No. Bring her with you."

She nodded.

The fact that Hope was coming convinced Brie that Sir was meeting with a mutual friend. Originally, she had assumed he would go to Rytsar because they were close like brothers. However, it now seemed Brie was mistaken, leaving her wondering who he had chosen to speak with.

As if he could read her mind, Sir told her, "While I speak with Gray, you can spend time visiting with Celestia."

"That's a wonderful idea, Sir!"

Discussing this with Gray made sense. The two men greatly respected each other, and Marquis had been able to help Sir in the past. It was not only his intuitive powers but the healing aspect of his skills with the flogger that made him an excellent choice.

Yet, Brie was still surprised.

Sir had kept the dark and sordid nature of his relationship with Lilly private from everyone but a few of his closest friends. Revealing something of this magnitude to Marquis Gray was exceedingly courageous on his part.

Brie could feel the tension in the car as they drove to their home. She placed her hand on Sir's thigh and felt him instantly relax.

"I'm grateful you are here," he told her.

"There is no other place I would rather be, Sir."

Marquis Gray and Celestia greeted them at the door when they arrived. The instant Celestia saw Hope, she smiled and held out her hands to the baby. "My, aren't you growing up fast!"

Even though Celestia was nearly a stranger to Hope, she responded to the woman's loving nature and reached out her little hands for her.

"I'm impressed," Sir stated. "Hope is a gregarious child, but it normally takes her a bit to warm up to new people."

"She and I have an understanding," Celestia laughed lightly. Hope started babbling at Celestia as if she could understand every word.

"You must," Brie agreed, tickled by their instant connection.

Marquis spoke to Sir in a somber tone. "Due to the seriousness of your visit, may I suggest we go to my office straight away?"

Sir glanced at Brie before nodding to him. "Let's."

Brie was struck once again by Marquis Gray's intimidating nature as she watched them walk down the hall. His uncanny ability to get straight to the heart of an issue made him both a strong ally and a man to be feared.

"While our men talk, why don't we go into the living room?" Celestia suggested. "I've set out treats for you both."

Brie blushed. "You didn't need to go to any trouble."

Celestia graced her with a beautiful smile. "It was my

pleasure, Brie. I always enjoy spending time with you, and having Hope here is an added gift."

"You are much too kind," Brie told her when she saw the plethora of homemade refreshments and the bowl of pickles thoughtfully cut up in tiny pieces for Hope.

"When Marquis informed me that Sir Davis had switched the meeting to today, I was so excited." She glanced down the hallway toward his office. "Although I understand this isn't a social call."

"Well, it is for us." Brie sat down on the floor next to the coffee table. Hope went straight for the pickles the moment Celestia set her down.

They chatted for a couple of minutes before Brie heard Sir's raised voice. She let out a nervous sigh.

"Don't worry, Brie. They'll be fine," Celestia assured her.

She nodded, popping a small candy into her mouth and chewing on it slowly, trying desperately not to worry.

A short time later, they heard both men raising their voices at each other.

Even Celestia looked concerned as she broke up a cookie for Hope.

As the yelling continued, the two women glanced at each other, smiling nervously. Both went for the plate of chocolate at the same time.

Suddenly, Sir burst out of the office with Marquis Gray following close behind him. Sir turned to face him and shouted, "You are infuriating!"

Marquis Gray narrowed his eyes. "Well, I've certainly been called worse."

"Good God, man!" Sir snarled. "I came here tonight looking for help, and you refuse to give it."

"What you came for was someone to agree with you," Marquis stated calmly, his eyes boring into Sir. "I am not that man and you know it. Therefore, you must ask yourself why you came to me when you *knew* my stance on the matter."

Sir glared at him. "I thought you were a friend."

Meeting his hostile gaze, Marquis Gray answered, "I am."

"Well, it fucking doesn't feel like it!"

Turning to Brie, Sir barked, "Get your things. We're leaving."

He swept Hope into his arms and waited impatiently for Brie.

Giving Celestia a worried glance, Brie quickly grabbed her purse and the diaper bag.

Sir took a moment to collect himself and then nodded to Celestia. "Thank you for your hospitality."

He placed his hand against Brie's back and briskly walked her toward the door.

"I will be here if you need me," Marquis Gray called out.

"Fuck you, Gray!" Sir yelled, slamming the door behind them.

Brie got into the car without saying a word. Sir shut the passenger door with considerable force once she was in, before strapping Hope into her car seat.

She had no idea why things had gone so badly between the two men and sat in silence, feeling numb.

Sir got into the car without saying a word and revved the engine before taking off.

Tears pricked Brie's eyes. She could sense the immense pain Sir was suffering after the unexpected confrontation.

Instead of gaining a sense of peace and a new perspective on Lilly, it appeared Sir's meeting with Marquis
had only made things considerably worse. That was
evident by the tightness of his clenched jaw and the
death grip he had on the steering wheel on the entire
drive home.

Brie was reminded of another car ride after Sir left
Marquis Gray's place in a similar state. Marquis had
confronted him about his care of Brie after learning Sir
had been cold and distant with her. At the time, Sir had
retreated into a dark place mentally and it almost destroyed him.

The heated words exchanged between the two men
that night had left Sir furious and defensive afterward.
Brie shuddered, remembering that awful car ride home
and how worried she'd been about Sir—and the stability
of their relationship.

But, the difference between then and now was like
night and day.

Over time, Brie had come to understand that if she
was patient and gave Sir space, he would calm down
enough to tell her what had happened. She knew the
only thing he needed from her at this moment was to
quietly support him while he processed through it. There
was no reason for her to fear.

That was the power of experience.

Understanding Sir on a much deeper level now, the
insecurities she once harbored had no place in their
relationship. As for Sir, he'd also wrestled through his
fears of not being a suitable partner because of his inner
demons. He'd eventually come to understand her need
for him to be open with her and vowed to always honor
it.

Brie glanced back at Hope with a sense of confidence, giving their daughter a reassuring smile.

They were condors.

There was nothing that could shake their foundation—no matter how great the force might be against them.

Toying with Her

After Sir's failed meeting with Marquis, Brie was even more anxious for Rytsar's return. Sir had remained silent about that night, but he was not acting distant with her or the baby.

Brie took that as a positive sign.

When Mary called, she was grateful for the distraction. "I've got some exciting news for you, Stinky Cheese."

"That's wonderful. What is it?"

"Come meet me at the coffee shop."

"Aww, come on. Don't leave me hanging like that, Mary."

"Sorry, Stinks. I'm not saying anything until I see you in person."

"Can't you give me a hint?"

"Fine, but only one. It has something to do with your first documentary."

Brie chuckled. "Well, that's the last thing I expected you to say."

"I know. It's pretty unprecedented. Don't take too long, bitch. I'm headed to the cafe now." Mary ended the call, leaving Brie hanging on the line.

She headed to Sir's office and knocked on the door-frame. The instant he looked up, his eyes softened. "What do you need, babygirl?"

"Mary just asked me to meet her at the coffee shop. She says she has something exciting to share about my first documentary, but I won't go if I'm needed here."

He encouraged her to meet with Mary. "Even if Miss Wilson's news amounts to nothing, it's obvious she needs you."

Brie stood there, admiring Sir.

"What?" he asked with an amused smile.

"You never stopped looking out for her."

"She not only was my charge once as the Headmaster of the Training Center, but she proved instrumental in protecting you from Lilly. She has earned my undying loyalty," he stated. "Go to her while I look after Hope. I suspect there may be something more to this invitation."

Brie walked over to hug him. "I'm extremely fortunate to be collared by such a man."

He chuckled sadly. "Not all fortune is good, my dear."

Brie knew he still held himself responsible for Lilly's actions even though he was not to blame. She hoped that Rytsar would help him gain a better perspective since his meeting with Marquis Gray had failed to do so.

Brie blew her daughter a kiss before walking out the door. She hoped Mary's news would give them all something small to celebrate.

Mary motioned her to the table at the café. The first thing Brie noticed was that Mary was wearing a pair of oversized sunglasses.

Brie found it odd and a little concerning.

As soon as Brie sat down, Mary pushed a cup of coffee to her. "You keep pissing off Greg, I'll have you know."

Brie frowned, now worried for her. "I haven't done anything."

"Well, whoever is backing you sure has."

Brie leaned in closer. "What's happened?"

"It appears your first documentary has suddenly gained critical acclaim and the word on the street has it that it'll be up for an award."

Brie sat back in her chair, shaking her head. "You're playing me."

Mary scoffed. "Like I would waste my time with that shit. I'm serious. Your documentary is being seriously considered for some honorary award for Most Compelling Living Subjects of a Documentary."

Brie smiled. "That's an award I'll gladly accept."

"You don't understand, Brie. Your film has been out for a while. This kind of thing doesn't happen."

Brie crinkled her brows. "Why do you think it is happening now?"

A sly smile spread across Mary's face. "I think whoever your secret admirer is wants to drum up attention for your first film."

"Why?"

"I'm sure it's to give the second documentary credentials when it's released. But I'm telling you, Brie, this move has Greg on a rampage."

Brie stared at Mary with concern. "Is that the reason

for the sunglasses?"

She growled, "What are you implying?"

Knowing she needed to tread lightly, Brie told her, "It just seems a little odd that you're wearing sunglasses inside the café, that's all."

Mary frowned and whipped her shades off. "I already told you. Greg would never damage the merchandise, if *that's* what you're getting at, bitch."

Brie was relieved to not see any bruises on Mary's beautiful face, but she didn't miss the dark circles under her eyes, which Mary had tried unsuccessfully to cover up with makeup.

Worried for her friend, she asked, "How are things going with him?"

Mary glanced around the café before leaning in close, her voice venomous. "I don't want to talk about it."

Brie nodded meekly. She picked up her mug and took a sip of her latte.

"Anyway," Mary continued, "even though this is a casual event among peers in the industry, I would still suggest dressing up for it."

Brie shook her head. "What event?"

"The one where you receive the award, idiot."

"You mean there's actually going to be an awards ceremony?"

"Nothing formal, but yeah. You will be recognized for the achievement during the event in front of everyone in attendance. I can't stress enough how important that is for you right now."

"Who else is going to be there?"

Mary rattled off several familiar names, including Finn. That was reason enough for Brie to attend, but she was still hesitant. "Is Holloway going to be there too?"

"No, he considers events like these beneath him."

"Good," Brie sighed in relief.

Mary grabbed her hand, squeezing it hard. "Don't be afraid to meet Greg face to face. He may be a powerhouse in Hollywood, but he has nothing on you. Don't you ever let him make you feel small."

Brie realized she needed to hear that and smiled gratefully at Mary.

Mary let go of her hand and asked smugly, "You plan to be there, right?"

Brie took another sip of her latte, then set it down before answering. "Only if you promise to go with me."

"I wouldn't miss it, Stinks."

"I guess I better ask when it is," Brie laughed.

"The event isn't for another month. Make sure your calendar is free. This move won't have near the same impact if you aren't there to receive the award in front of all those fuckers sucking up to Greg."

"I'm sure whoever is championing my film will be there, don't you think?"

Mary huffed. "I'd be surprised if they were. Although this event is too pedestrian for Greg, he'll have his minions on the hunt. He's determined to annihilate the enemy by any means necessary." She paused, adding, "I guess I can't blame him…"

Brie frowned. "Why would you say that?"

"If your secret admirer succeeds, Greg will be done in this town. He's put his entire reputation on the line and there will be no coming back from this." Mary's eyes flashed with the need for revenge. "I'm praying for that day."

"I can't wait! No one should hold that kind of power over people."

Mary let out a worried sigh. "That's something that's got me a little concerned."

"Why?"

"Whoever this secret admirer is, he or she has that kind of power, Stinks. I wouldn't trust whoever it is if I were you."

Brie chuckled lightly as she thought of Finn. "I think you're just being paranoid."

Mary looked her straight in the eye. "No, I'm not. Don't forget, I speak from personal experience. Secret admirers are the Devil's spawn."

Brie looked at her with sympathy.

"You know one of the things I hate the most?" Mary shook her head vehemently. "I know I said I didn't want to talk about Greg, but that fucker stole the magic of Disney from me. It's the only thing that kept me sane all of these years, and now..." She slipped her sunglasses back on and picked up her cup of coffee, sipping it silently.

She remembered how shocked she'd been when she learned Holloway was the one who left the movies on Mary's doorstep as a child.

Brie could only imagine the loss Mary felt having that cherished part of her childhood ripped away, remembering the multitude of Disney figurines that used to line Mary's apartment.

"Greg not only took away my future," she said with a catch in her voice, "but the only thing I loved about my past."

It angered Brie. "No! Holloway does not get to have that kind of power over you. Your love of Disney helped shape you into the person you are today. It's one of the quirky things I like about you. The only thing that monster did was introduce you to the films. You are the one who internalized the positive messages you found in them and used them to survive. *You* did that. Fuck that asshole. He doesn't get to claim any part of it from you."

Mary sat back in her chair. "Wow, Stinks. I think someone here may have had one too many shots of espresso."

Brie took a deep breath, trying to calm herself. "I just don't want you to lose that part of yourself, damn it!"

Mary took another sip of her coffee. With her shades on, her expression was unreadable. "I'll take that under advisement."

Brie looked at her friend with compassion. "I love you, Mary."

Mary smirked. "Good God, Brie. Don't go declaring your love for me after your little outburst." She looked around the room in pretend shame.

Brie rolled her eyes, spotting traces of Blonde Nemesis peeking through. Mary always backed away whenever she felt people were getting too real. Still, Brie was grateful she'd come.

Sir had been right, Mary needed her.

But, the truth was, Brie needed her just as much.

Brie was relieved to hear Rytsar was returning to the States. Sir made a special request that he join them on the night of his return.

The Russian was unusually late that evening despite having flown in early in the afternoon.

"Do you think something is wrong, Sir?" she asked

worriedly, looking at the clock.

Sir raised an eyebrow. "He may be dealing with an issue a certain duo left for him."

Brie blushed, having forgotten about the humorous prank. "I sure hope he can forgive me."

"We'll find out soon enough," he chuckled.

Rytsar arrived a full hour later than expected. Brie was nervous. She fully expected him to barge into their house demanding an explanation from her.

Instead, he came bearing gifts for all three of them— an elaborate Staunton chess board with inlaid wood and hand-carved chess pieces for Sir, a sweet child's tea set made of wood with tiny flowers painted on them for Hope, and an exquisite Russian lacquer music box for her.

When Brie wound it up and opened the lid, she was moved to tears on hearing the haunting melody of *Pas de Deux* from Tchaikovsky's *The Nutcracker*.

"I love this, Rytsar."

His eyes flashed with approval. "I have always been fond of this particular song."

"Well, I certainly didn't expect to receive gifts on a fact-finding mission for Lilly," Sir stated as he looked over each chess piece with admiration.

"I am a man of passion, *moy droog,* and need no excuse to give gifts."

He turned to Brie and said with a glint in his eyes. "Don't you agree, *radost moya?*"

Brie forced herself to play it cool when she answered—even though she suspected she was about to be interrogated by the Russian about the prank. "Yes. Gifts given from the heart are always cherished."

"Particularly when they are unexpected," he added.

Brie knew he was leading her to confess, but she'd promised Master Anderson to admit to nothing and replied, "Those are the best kind."

"*Da...*" He gazed into her eyes. She was held captive by that intense blue gaze and fought hard not to crumble under it.

"What's wrong, *radost moya?*" Rytsar inquired with a sly grin. "You look as if you have something to say."

She suddenly held up the music box and smiled. "It's so pretty. Thank you."

He leaned in closer, pinning her against the wall. "Is that really what you want to tell me?"

Brie let out a nervous giggle. "I can't express how grateful I am you're back."

He stared deep into her eyes, demanding more.

She held her breath, her heart racing. Brie was close to breaking under his intense stare, and silently chided herself for taunting the sadist.

What the hell was I thinking?

"I hear there is news about your film."

Brie let her breath out slowly, unprepared for the question. Realizing she was safe for the moment, she smiled at him beguilingly. "Mary told me that some unknown entity has been gathering a dream team in Hollywood, and she suspects it has everything to do with my second documentary—although no one has been able to confirm it. It's crazy, because the entire thing has been shrouded in mystery. No one in Hollywood is willing to publicly cross Greg Holloway. But the best part is that it looks like my original documentary will be receiving an honorary award."

Rytsar slapped his hands against the wall beside her head, making her jump. "That is excellent news, *radost moya!*"

"It is!" Brie grinned with excitement, spurred on by his enthusiasm.

"You wouldn't happen to know who that might be?" Sir asked him.

Rytsar grinned, his eyes sparkling with mischief. "I do not, *moy droog*. However, when I discover who it is, I will show them my gratitude—personally."

"Don't you find it strange that they've been able to keep it a secret?" Sir asked.

The Russian shrugged. "With enough money, anything is possible…"

Sir raised an eyebrow. "Agreed, and there's only one person I know who has that kind of money."

Rytsar chuckled, a grin spreading across his face. "It's not me, *moy droog*. Unfortunately, having no experience with the inner workings of Hollywood, I've made little progress in that area."

Brie smiled, hearing his confession. "So, you *have* been trying."

Rytsar snorted. "Of course! I am invested in this film on several fronts. Not only do I believe in the message of the film, but I have an important role in it. Besides, I happen to love the director."

She blushed, touched by his declaration.

"Well, if it's not you, then who?" Sir pressed.

Brie decided to reveal her benefactor. "I believe it's Finn. Although I don't have any solid evidence, he respects my work and has a reputation for being a rebel in Hollywood."

"Didn't he refuse to meet with you even after you sat in his office for over a week?" Sir reminded her.

"He did, Sir. However, I understand why now. Finn

must show a pretense of solidarity with Holloway or he risks being blacklisted in Hollywood."

"I would like to speak to this Finn person," Rytsar stated.

"Please don't!" she begged. "Not yet. I could never forgive myself if we inadvertently brought attention to him and destroyed his career."

Rytsar tilted his head, frowning slightly, but said, "As you wish, *radost moya*."

He turned his attention on Sir. "Shall we discuss what is distressing you, comrade?"

Sir let out an exasperated sigh. "Am I that obvious?"

Rytsar laughed in answer. "Come, sit."

Sir gestured for Brie to join him on the couch and explained what happened during his recent confrontation with Marquis Gray.

Rytsar interrupted. "Why did you go to that man?"

"Ironically, he asked me the same question." Sir chuckled with irritation.

"*Moy droog*, Gray does not understand the seriousness of the situation. All his moral ideals have no place here."

Letting out a long sigh, Sir admitted, "It was the point of contention between us."

"Do not be troubled," he assured Sir. "We both know the woman is dangerously unstable. Dr. Volkov confirmed it with extensive testing."

"True. I was not surprised by the doctor's findings," Sir conceded.

"You know what must be done, and I am the man to do it."

Dread washed over Brie. The moment she had agonized over was playing out before her very eyes. "We can't."

Rytsar looked Brie dead in the eye. "I will not lose

you or the babe to such evil."

"Brother," Sir said gruffly, pain lacing his voice. "I want Lilly dead as well because I'm not willing to risk the life of my wife or children, but…"

"But what?" Rytsar demanded.

"Marquis said something that still resonates with me. If I make this one moral concession—no matter how justified—I will eventually become like my mother and Lilly."

Sir turned to Brie. "Gray said he saw it clear as day."

Chills ran down Brie's spine.

"When Gray did not give me the answer I wanted, I asked him for a session with the flogger. I needed the pain to disappear, if only for a moment."

Brie nodded, understanding completely.

"But, he denied me even that," he snarled. "Gray said he refused to act as my pain addiction."

She sucked in her breath, remembering when Marquis Gray told her the same thing at the Collaring Ceremony.

"Why would he tell you that?" Rytsar snorted. "You are no masochist."

"No, I am not." Sir closed his eyes. "However, he was right."

"*Moy droog…*" Rytsar protested.

Sir opened his eyes, his expression pained when he admitted, "My primal instinct is to kill Lilly and eliminate the threat to my family—but I fear it will change me. I believe that is the reason I sought out Gray's counsel."

"Oh, Sir," Brie cried, reaching out to him in support.

Agony hardening his expression, he confessed, "It seems I must risk losing my family or I will become the very thing I want to kill. Neither choice is acceptable to me."

Firsts

S ir asked Brie to invite Faelan and Kylie to join them for an afternoon on the beach. "It would be good for me to get Wallace's perspective on the situation, and I'm sure Kylie would appreciate time relaxing in the sun before her life is no longer hers."

Brie laughed. "She has no idea what she's in for. Her life will never be the same." Glancing at Hope, she added, "But, I have no regrets."

He put his arm around her, gazing at their daughter. "No regrets."

When the two arrived, Brie headed to the beach with Kylie and Hope so the two men could talk privately about Lilly. She noticed Kylie was already showing. "How far along are you?"

She giggled, looking down at her small baby bump. "Turns out I'm four months. Doctor Glas says the baby is healthy and is progressing well."

"So, you did decide to go with my pediatrician." Brie said, pleased to hear it.

"I did, and I do enjoy his Scottish accent! He's been incredibly patient with me and my hundreds of questions."

"Dr. Glas is great. I loved having him as my doctor for Hope and I'm grateful that he'll be delivering our next baby, too."

"So, you're about one month along, right?" she asked.

"Yep. Sounds like I'm a trimester behind you."

"I'm happy we're in this together, Brie."

"Me, too. We can share all the crazy little things that happen during pregnancy."

Brie led Kylie out to the sunshade that Sir had already set up. Putting Hope on the beach blanket, Brie handed her a toy shovel and bucket to play with. Hope immediately began banging them together.

"While we enjoy the sun, she'll get to stay safe under the shade," she told Kylie.

"She's such a lucky girl." Kylie sat down on the low beach chair and laughed. "You know, I have no idea what I am going to do when I am eight months pregnant. I can't believe how much my body is changing."

Brie giggled. "You have so many changes ahead, girl. Our bodies metamorphosize into baby-making machines. It's like you become part of a miracle, and when you feel them move inside you…" She sighed happily. "It's pure magic."

Kylie's eyes lit up. "I didn't know what that feeling was at first. It was like a little flutter. And then, when I realized it was the baby, I tried to get Faelan to feel it."

Brie grinned. "Yeah, he won't be able to feel it for a little longer."

"Well, we spent hours trying." Kylie laughed, then turned to the ocean and let out a satisfied sigh. "I'm so happy right now I can hardly stand it."

Brie loved hearing that. "I'm happy for you both."

"So, I do have a couple of questions…"

Brie spent the next hour answering all of Kylie's many questions. It was nice to be the experienced one this time around.

"Do you have any food cravings?"

"Not yet." Kylie sounded a bit disappointed. "However, I can't stand the smell of garlic and I've always loved that smell. What's up with that?"

"Pregnancy hormones can cause crazy things." Brie giggled. "Luckily, I haven't experienced that one myself. With Sir's Italian background, it would be a rough nine months in the kitchen if I couldn't stand the smell of garlic."

Kylie grinned. "I have to say Faelan has been amazing—so attentive and caring. You really get to know a man on a different level when you carry his baby."

"Agreed."

They soaked up the rays of the sun as they continued to chat. Eventually, their men came out to join them.

"What are you two up to? Plotting world domination?" Faelan joked.

Kylie rubbed her tummy, smiling up at him. "One baby at a time."

Brie closed her eyes as they all lay listening to the waves, enjoying the warmth of the sun.

Faelan broke the pleasant silence. "As far as your situation with Lilly…I think there is something you need to consider."

Sir turned his head toward him. "And what would that be?"

"Faith."

Sir snorted. "What do you mean by that?"

"If you end the threat, you know the path it will lead you down. Based on that alone, you have to choose the alternative and have faith."

Sir grunted. "I am not a man of faith."

Brie reached out to him. "I wouldn't say that, Sir."

"It's true," he insisted. "I have zero faith in the future, only in what I can control."

"I'm surprised you haven't learned that lesson by now." Faelan chuckled. "Any control you think you have is only an illusion."

Sir shook his head. "I wholeheartedly disagree."

"Take me for example," Faelan continued. "I thought I was going to be a famous football star and sacrificed everything for it, but look at me now." He held out his hand to Kylie to squeeze it. "Funny thing is, I wouldn't change it for the world. Even losing this." He tapped the patch covering his eye.

"I believe life is a series of choices. We go down paths of our own making, but there is an element of the unknown that influences our lives."

"How very philosophical of you," Sir stated. "But that has no place in my world."

Faelan smirked. "Or it does, but you are unwilling to accept it."

Sir shook his head, chuckling with amusement.

When it came time for Faelan and Kylie to leave, Sir collapsed the sunshade and they walked back to the house.

Faelan dropped his car keys, and Sir knelt to pick them up.

"Sir…" Brie said in awe as Hope took her first steps toward him.

He turned to look and held out his hands to her.

Hope was so excited that she lost her balance and tumbled to the floor.

Unfazed, she pulled herself up using the couch and tried again.

"You can do it," he encouraged as she took several uncertain steps toward him. Sir met her halfway and scooped her into his arms. "Good job, little angel."

Brie rushed over, gushing. "You did it! You're such a big girl." Grinning at Sir, she said, "I was too excited to get it on video."

"Never fear." Faelan held up his phone. "I got it."

"Thank you, Faelan!"

Brie covered Hope in kisses before Sir set her down on the floor and let her try again. Her heart melted when she noticed Faelan taking Kylie's hand as the two watched Hope slowly make her way across the floor.

It was a poignant moment.

"Would you guys like to come to Hope's birthday?" Brie asked. "We're having a small gathering but would love it if you could come."

Kylie glanced at Faelan and grinned. When he nodded, she answered, "We'd love to."

"No need for gifts," Sir told them.

"What?" Kylie laughed. "Can't we buy her anything?"

Brie grinned. "Since Hope has everything she needs as a one-year-old, we decided no gifts this year. But you can donate to Baby2Baby in her name if you'd like. They provide children with diapers, clothing, and other basic necessities."

"We'll be happy to contribute. Shoot me the link," Faelan said, opening the front door for Kylie. "When is the party?"

"Next Saturday at three," Sir answered.

After they left, Brie rushed back to Hope and cooed. "Now, show Mommy just how many steps you can take."

Brie stood back to stare at the pink and purple streamers, multiple flower balloons, and twinkling fairy lights. Bumping shoulders with Lea, she said, "Not too bad, eh?"

"Not too bad?" Lea snorted. "We've created a virtual fairyland for Hope. Makes me wish I could be a kid again."

"I bet you were cute back then," Brie mused. She looked around the room and muttered, "Now, where did I put that present for Jonathan?"

"I think it's hilarious you insist on no gifts for Hope, but you're giving Jonathan a present."

"Hope is going to be the center of attention today. I think it's only fair that Jonathan feels special, too."

Lea wrapped her arms around her, pressing her big boobs against Brie's chest. "And that's why you make such a great mom."

Brie stared at Lea tenderly, overcome with emotion. "I love you, Lea."

"Same here, Stinky Cheese. I think this calls for something special."

Brie waved her finger back and forth. "I'm not drinking, remember?"

"I wasn't talking about booze, girlfriend," Lea giggled. "I hear you're having a new baby."

"Yeah…"

"What's wrong with the old one?"

Brie rolled her eyes. "Was that supposed to be a joke?"

Lea grinned. "Hey, Brie?"

"What?" she groaned, waiting for the next one.

"If a baby refuses to go to sleep…" Lea paused for a moment, then looked up, tapping her finger on her chin as if she were thinking. "…is he resisting arrest?"

Brie giggled.

Seeing she was on a roll, Lea continued. "Hey, Brie?"

Realizing she must be a masochist at heart, Brie played her part. "What?"

"Who's bigger? Mrs. Bigger, Mr. Bigger, or their baby?"

"I don't know."

"Their baby—because he's a little Bigger."

Brie snorted. "Where do you come up with these?"

Lea winked. "I've got one more. So, there's this dad who tries to keep his wife happy through labor by telling a bunch of jokes, but she doesn't laugh—not even once. Do you know why?"

"Because the jokes are terrible?" Brie answered in a deadpan voice.

"No silly. Because it was the delivery!"

Brie slapped her palm to her head, chuckling despite herself.

"What's so funny?" Sir asked, walking through the room.

"Lea's telling me jokes."

"And you're laughing?" Sir's comeback was quick and unexpected, catching them both off guard.

Lea put her hands to her heart, a tragic expression on

her face. "That hurt, Sir."

"Ms. Taylor, while I'm sure they were of the utmost quality, I have yet to find any of your jokes funny."

Sir delivered his humorous retort in such a matter-of-fact manner, it reminded Brie of the critiques he used to give at the Training Center.

Lea stared at him in disbelief as he walked away.

Brie threw her head back and started laughing. She couldn't stop. Every time she looked at Lea, she broke out in a fresh peal of laughter.

It wasn't until the doorbell rang that Brie was able to finally gather herself. Heading to the door, she wiped her eyes before welcoming in Mr. and Mrs. Reynolds and little Jonathan.

"I'm so tickled you guys could make it."

"Nothing could keep us away from Hope's first birthday," Judy told her, bouncing Jonathan in her arms.

Jack glanced around. "Where is the birthday girl?"

"She's just waking from her nap. Sir will be down in a bit. Can I get you any refreshments while you wait?"

Judy stopped to admire the decorations. "Oh, Brie. I love what you've done. It's so festive and sweet.

Brie winked at Lea. "We had fun setting it up."

"You two always have fun together," Jack observed, smiling at them both.

When he set Jonathan down on the floor, the little boy stood there clinging to Mr. Reynold's leg, staring at Lea shyly.

Brie spied the gift on the counter and grabbed it. Kneeling beside him she said, "This is for you, Jonathan."

The little boy looked up at her with his big brown eyes and long lashes. Those eyes, along with his classic good looks, left no doubt that he was Lilly's son. Although it was disconcerting for Brie, she felt only love for this innocent boy.

She stood back and watched with joy as Sir's uncle helped Jonathan unwrap the gift. Mr. Reynolds opened the box and handed Jonathan one of the colorful balls inside.

Brie explained, "The elephant shoots the balls out of his trunk whenever Jonathan presses the button."

"Oh, he's going to love that," Judy exclaimed excitedly.

"I thought he would enjoy chasing them."

After he set the elephant on the floor, he filled it with the other balls and held Jonathan's hand to help him press the button. The elephant began playing a happy little tune as a green ball shot across the floor.

Jonathan's eyes widened and he squealed as he toddled off to get it.

"I think you have a winner there," Sir said from behind her.

Brie turned and saw Hope dressed in the frilly dress she had picked out for the big day. The yellow dress had a puffy fairy skirt with a big satin bow in the back. She looked just like a ray of sunshine.

"Hello, birthday girl!" Brie cooed.

Hope reached out to her and let Brie cuddle for a moment. However, she was entranced by the elephant and was soon squirming in Brie's arms, wanting to be put down. As soon as she saw Jonathan, she completely forgot about the elephant.

Hope was entranced by her cousin as he toddled to her, and she stared at him with open adoration.

Brie had to excuse herself from the adorable moment to answer the doorbell again.

Soon the house was filled with the guests she had invited to the small celebration, including Mary, Mr. Gallant and his family, and Celestia and Marquis Gray. Despite their heated confrontation recently, Sir and Marquis Gray were cordial to each other, acting as if nothing had happened.

Only one person was missing—Hope's *dyadya*.

When Rytsar came, he burst into the house without waiting for Brie to answer the door and called out, "Where is my favorite girl?"

Hope looked up and smiled, squeaking with delight as he approached her. He was carrying a large box wrapped in a purple bow.

"We said no gifts," Sir reminded him.

Rytsar scoffed. "I am her *dyadya*. I follow no rules." He pulled a check from his breast pocket and handed it to Brie. "For the other babes."

She unfolded it, surprised to see it was for ten thousand dollars. "That is going to help a lot of babies!"

He winked at her, before sitting down on the floor beside Hope. Pushing the box toward her, he exclaimed, "Happy first birthday, *moye solntse*."

Just like at Christmas, Hope was far more interested in the pretty bow on the package than the present itself. But Rytsar found it charming as he unwrapped the gift for her.

Pulling out a large cloth box, he placed it in front of Hope, then reached into the opening on top and pulled out a stuffed butterfly with crinkly wings. Rytsar handed it to her and reached into the box again. This time, he pulled out a fuzzy sunflower with a mirrored surface for the center. Each item he pulled out of the box had a different texture and shape, including a white pony with a long mane. He stuffed them back into the box and shook it before sliding it toward her.

Hope grinned as she stuck her hand into the top of the cloth box and pulled out a fuzzy violin. She squeezed it and the toy squeaked, making her giggle.

The smile on Sir's face touched Brie. He patted Rytsar on the back before turning to their friends. "Shall we light the candle?"

Everyone gathered around Hope as Brie brought out the cake, which looked like a miniature fairy garden.

Several of the ladies "oohed" and "ahhed" as she set it on the table. Sir lit the candle in the center of the garden and Brie waited a moment singing, "Happy birthday to you…"

Brie looked around the room, smiling to herself as all of the Doms in attendance joined in, singing the simple song in honor of Hope. Remembering her first night at the Submissive Training Center, Brie could never have imagined such a thing—not in a million years.

It was a testament to the close-knit family they had built in this community.

She gazed lovingly at her daughter, who refused to let go of the violin, even though she was mesmerized by the candle on the pretty cake.

Brie felt as if Alonzo was with them and she knew he would be proud of his little granddaughter. She wondered if Hope's natural affinity for the instrument might manifest itself later on in her life.

Leaning toward the cake, Brie and Sir blew out the candle together.

Rytsar walked up and threw his arm around Sir while Brie was cutting the cake. He smiled down at their little girl. "*Moye solntse* will have the childhood you and I never had, brother. She will know the love of both parents and will meet the world with joy."

Sir stared at Brie tenderly. "That she will, old friend."

Slaying Them

Brie had started taking long walks in the early morning. Walking beside the ocean as the sun slowly dawned had become a cherished part of her day.

During those daily walks, she crossed paths with an older homeless woman at the same garbage can each morning. The woman had an adorable furry mutt with matted hair. It wagged its tail eagerly and sniffed the can while she collected the plastic bottles from it.

Brie always greeted the woman with a cheerful smile and a wave as she passed, although the woman never returned the smile.

Seeing them at the same time each day became part of her morning routine. Brie was moved to help her and had offered the woman money on two separate occasions, but she was vehemently turned down both times.

While Brie admired her strong work ethic and didn't want to insult the woman, she became concerned when she noticed the dog was losing patches of hair.

The woman's distress over her ailing companion was easy to see by the way she kept constantly glancing at her little dog as she retrieved the plastic bottles from the trash can. It troubled Brie enough to speak to Sir about it when she returned home.

"I really want to help her, Sir, but I've tried in the past with no success."

He closed his laptop and looked up at her. "I can understand her position. I felt that way once. When you've been forced to be independent for so long, accepting help feels like you've failed somehow."

"But she needs help. I can't just keep walking by every morning and watch her little dog slowly die, Sir."

He glanced briefly at Shadow before meeting her gaze. "Find a way to give it to her anonymously and she may be more receptive to it."

Brie nodded, grateful for his insight. "I'll do that, Sir. I don't know how, but I'll find a way."

He took her hand and squeezed it. "I am certain you will."

Sir insisted on taking Brie shopping for the award ceremony coming up. "This is an important moment in your career. I suspect you will be met with fear and resentment from your peers. However, you will stand before them in confidence. I want you to slay them, babygirl."

His confidence in her reinforced her determination to act as the victor and not one of Holloway's victims when she took the stage to receive her award. With that in mind, she entered the high-end shop determined to find the perfect dress.

Brie was treated like royalty. She sipped her mock

champagne and chatted with Sir while they sat in white leather chairs. Meanwhile, the wardrobe stylist walked through the shop, singling out designer dresses for her to try on.

"I think this one will be stunning on you," he told her, showing Brie a purple sequined gown.

Brie left Sir's side and smiled while two women followed her into the luxurious changing room to help her into the dress. She gazed at the three-paneled mirror and turned slowly. The gown clung to her curves, and the low cut of the bodice showed off her cleavage nicely. She was grateful the event was fast approaching because she wouldn't be showing yet, so there would be no need to have the dress altered.

She walked out to show Sir, who smiled as soon as laid his eyes on her. "Turn for me."

Brie turned slowly, enjoying his critical gaze as he assessed the dress. She was not surprised when he shook his head no.

"I agree, Sir." She looked at her reflection. "It would be perfect for a party, but not as a statement."

"Exactly," he agreed.

Listening to their comments, the stylist picked out a new dress that was bright red and angular in its cut. Brie walked out and slowly spun for Sir, basking in his attention as he studied every curve of the dress.

"Your thoughts?" he asked her.

Brie smiled as she looked at the mirror. "I actually think it is too much of a statement. I feel like a stern businesswoman in this dress."

"Agreed," he replied, "although it is a flattering look on you."

She blushed. "Thank you, Sir."

The stylist looked her over once more and nodded to himself. "I know which one will kill it," he declared as he left them to get the dress.

Sir handed her the champagne flute. "Having fun, my dear?"

Brie grinned as she took a sip. "I feel like a princess."

"You are far more than a princess." Cradling her cheek, he gazed at her in admiration. "You are my téa."

Goddess…

"You make me feel like one, Master," she said breathlessly, closing her eyes as he leaned in for a kiss. Brie almost dropped her glass as she gave in to the passion of his kiss.

The stylist stood quietly waiting until Sir released her. Holding up a royal blue dress, he told her, "Blue denotes truth and wisdom. It is also linked to intellect and has a calming effect over others."

"I might need that," Brie laughed. "I'm expecting to walk into the lion's den."

"This should work perfectly, Mrs. Davis," he stated with confidence.

She left to try on the dress and felt a surge of excitement when the lady helping to zip it up let out a gasp and stepped back to look at Brie.

Glancing at the mirror, Brie felt tingles of providence as she gazed at the gown. The dress had a wide V-neck that showed off her shoulders but did not dip down low enough to make her cleavage a distraction. The three-quarter length sleeves gave it a professional look, along with the tight waist and the alluring slit in the skirt. The cut of the dress was both feminine and sharp. A real showstopper.

Brie walked out to Sir, carrying herself with an air of

self-assurance that she knew was inspired by the dress. As soon as he saw her, his eyes widened and he stood up. "Turn…"

She turned slowly, smiling at him the entire time.

"Not only does the color suit you, but it brings out the honey color of your eyes."

"Do you like it, Sir?" she asked, loving the dress.

"No."

Brie looked at him in surprise.

"'Like' is not a word I would use for this dress. You look stunning, babygirl. Absolutely stunning."

She threw her arms around his neck and stood on tiptoe to kiss him. "I feel like I could conquer the world in this dress."

"And you shall," he answered, pressing his lips against hers.

"Should I wrap it up for you, then?" the stylist asked, sounding pleased.

"Yes, along with the other two."

Brie's eyes widened. "Sir?"

"You looked striking in all three dresses. I would hate to part with any of them."

The stylist's smile grew. "Wonderful."

He turned to Brie. "You make any dress look eye-catching, Mrs. Davis."

"You're being too modest," she said, chuckling lightly. "It was your talent as a stylist. Thank you."

"It was my pleasure."

Brie stared lovingly at Sir after the stylist left the room. "How did I get so lucky?"

He held out his hand to her. "I ask myself that same question every day."

With an outfit that would silence her cynics, Brie was

set to face her next hurdle.

The night of the event, Brie felt a calm she had never experienced before. Despite the humiliation of having Holloway blacklist her, she knew she would become the victor. Tonight was the first step toward her return.

Brie walked into the hotel where the event was being held with an air of confidence. With Sir and Mary by her side, she felt protected. Having a silent ally in the audience made her a force to be reckoned with.

Knowing there was someone in the industry who had her back was humbling—and incredibly empowering.

Finn had made this moment possible, but could not publicly take the credit. There was something fantastically heroic about it, and Brie was determined to repay him in the years ahead.

In keeping with the pretense of siding with Holloway, Finn kept his distance from Brie, as did every other person in the room. People made a wide berth around her as if she were infected with the plague. They refused to look her in the eye, afraid of being seen even looking at her.

It was humorous to Brie, so she had fun with it. With a tiny smirk on her lips, she walked about the room making them scatter on purpose. It reminded her of walking through a flock of pigeons on the ground.

When it finally came time to announce the awards, Brie sat down with Sir and Mary at a table in the front. No one joined them. Only the hotel staff interacted with the three of them while serving food.

Brie glanced around the room, thinking how surreal it was to see professional men and women acting like scared children.

Sir put his hand on hers.

She smiled at him, unfazed by the callous treatment. It was to be expected in an industry ripe with exploitation and fear.

Mary leaned in and whispered, "You are knocking it out of the park, Stinks. Who'd have guessed that timid little girl I met on the first day of training would turn into the woman I see now?" She sat back in her seat staring at Brie proudly.

"I have to admit, I never would have guessed the Blonde Nemesis would end up becoming one of my dearest friends."

Mary picked up her wine glass, snickering. "The world sure is a fucked up place." She glanced at Sir having momentarily forgotten her place and immediately apologized. "Please excuse my language, Sir Davis."

He nodded. "Apology accepted. I, for one, agree with your assessment."

Mary smiled to herself and took another sip of her wine just as the ceremony began.

Brie clapped along with everyone else as all the winners walked up to receive their awards. She clapped even louder when Finn accepted the prestigious Landmark Award.

When she finally heard her name called, it felt as if time stood still. Brie glanced at Mary and then Sir and smiled.

She stood up feeling like the queen of the world.

Brie took her time, walking slowly as silence enveloped the room. No one made a sound as she ascended the stairs and took the plaque that the emcee handed to her.

She turned to face the assembly and smiled warmly at the crowd, unaffected by their icy silence.

This was *her* moment.

Glancing at Sir, she gave him a grateful nod before beginning her speech. "I am honored to receive this award tonight. This documentary sprang from my need to share my deep respect and passion for BDSM. But the award for Most Compelling Living Subjects of a Documentary is not about the lifestyle. Instead, it recognizes the people who practice it."

Brie paused and scanned the room, wanting them to hear her next words.

"In a world full of pressure to meet archaic societal norms, BDSM brings a healthy alternative to those who are open-minded. No longer forced into the shadows of society, this film celebrates people who are courageous enough to be true to themselves and their sexual desires. There is no shame in embracing the entirety of who we are and living out that truth with like-minded people. Shame only comes to those who are afraid of what they will find when they face their secret desires. I believe that is what drives their need to cast BDSM and those who practice it in a bad light."

Brie held up the plaque. "So, I am happy to accept this award for everyone who participated in the documentary and for all those courageous souls who live out this dynamic every day in their real lives. Here's to living a full and authentic life!"

Sir and Mary stood up and started clapping, while the entire assembly watched in hostile silence.

Then, from far across the room, one person stood up to join Sir and Mary, clapping his hands loudly. Brie was shocked when she saw who it was.

Darius…

The boy who had traumatized her as a child was the only one who was brave enough to acknowledge her now—possibly end his budding acting career.

In that moment, she felt a profound connection to him. While she could never forget what he'd done to her in the past, she admired the man he'd become.

Brie left the stage, exuding elegance and poise, holding her head high, but at a respectful angle as she approached Sir.

"Magnificent," he said as he helped her back to her seat.

Brie felt invincible as she scanned the room and caught several people staring at her despite themselves.

Message received, she thought.

On their way out, she saw Finn outside the hotel by himself, taking a smoke. Looking around to make sure no one was watching, she asked Sir and Mary to wait while she spoke to him.

"Finn, I just want to say how gratef—"

"What the hell is wrong with you? You've been following me around like a puppy the whole evening. It's pathetic," he snarled with disgust, throwing his cigarette to the ground and crushing it with his foot. "I have zero interest in you or anything you have to say. Your little stunt tonight accomplished nothing. Get the hell away from me…"

Finn turned his back on her and walked back into the hotel.

Brie stood there for a moment, stunned.

It hadn't been Finn, after all…

She walked back to Sir and Mary, rocked by the revelation.

"What did Finn have to say, babygirl?"

She looked up at him and frowned. "He's firmly in Holloway's camp."

"I could have told you that," Mary snorted. "Did you really think he was the one behind all this? You're going to have to think way bigger, woman. Someone like Finn doesn't have the influence or the balls to go against Holloway."

Brie sighed. "I guess it doesn't matter."

Looking back at the hotel she smiled, feeling the thrill of victory. "None of them had power over me tonight, and now they know it."

Sir wrapped his arm around her. It was evident how proud he was of her.

"You slayed them all, babygirl."

Precious Gifts

B rie was still flying high from her success the night before when she set out on her morning walk.

When she came across the old woman and her little dog, she waved enthusiastically to her and was greeted with a frown. With a flash of inspiration, Brie suddenly knew what she could do to help.

After returning home, she spoke with the vet clinic they used for Shadow, knowing it would be within walking distance for the old woman. The staff there were amazingly kind and open to Brie's idea. Together, they worked out the details and payment plan so that any of the bills would go to Brie.

She then jumped onto her computer and created an official-looking coupon for a free vet checkup. Knowing the woman didn't accept handouts, this seemed like the perfect solution to get the dog the care it needed without making the woman feel beholden to anyone. The receptionist was prepared to receive the coupon as if it were an everyday occurrence, and she assured Brie they would make sure the dog was well taken care of.

Satisfied the little dog would get the help it needed,

Brie decided to concentrate on the woman herself. Brie wanted to give her something but realized the item had to be practical and small or the woman wouldn't accept it.

Unsure what homeless people actually needed, Brie googled it and was excited to find a website detailing the most needed items for the homeless. Interestingly, socks were on the top of the list. It wasn't something Brie had even considered, but it made sense to her, knowing how much the woman walked each day gathering plastic bottles to redeem for cash.

Taking Hope with her to the store, Brie stared at the large display of socks, unsure about which pair to buy. "Should we go practical or cute?" she asked, holding up two different pairs of socks to Hope. One was plain white with a reinforced toe and heel, while the other was purple and had pretty daisies printed on it.

"What do you think, sweet pea?"

Hope naturally went for the colorful one.

"That's what I was thinking, too," Brie agreed. She went to put the plain ones back but suddenly had second thoughts. "Maybe I'll get both and let her decide." In the checkout line, she noticed a squeaky dog toy and quickly added it to her purchases.

Knowing the woman's routine, Brie decided the safest place to leave the gifts anonymously was in the trash bin itself. The old woman was guaranteed to look inside it when other people would not.

But, to make sure she received it. Brie would have to leave extra early to drop it off. Waking up an hour early the next morning, Brie quietly slipped out of bed, giddy with excitement.

She dressed in the dark, and was about to head out

the bedroom door when she heard Sir say, "Come here."

Brie immediately turned and approached the bed, unhappy that in her excitement, she had unknowingly woken him.

Sir reached up and caressed her cheek in the dark. "It is a beautiful thing you are doing."

"Thank you, Sir."

Pulling her closer, he planted a warm kiss on her lips. "I plan to reward you when you return."

Brie's heart fluttered at the thought. "I'm looking forward to it."

He lightly grazed her breast with his fingertips before letting her go. "I'll be thinking of you while I wait."

Just like that, he had her entire body humming with sexual desire. She smiled at him in the dark before leaving to grab her little package and head out.

Brie walked on the path lit up with streetlights, going straight to the garbage can. She carefully placed the gift and coupon, wrapped in red paper, into the trash bin with a note attached that read, *Help for Your Dog.* She placed an empty water bottle beside it so there was no chance the woman would miss it.

Brie then returned home and took her walk at the normal time, not wanting to alter her routine in any way that might incite suspicion. But, in her excitement, she must have walked a little faster because the woman wasn't there when she passed by the trash can.

Thankfully, Brie spotted her in the parking lot near-by, heading toward the can with her little dog.

Brie waved, calling out a cheery hello like normal and the woman frowned like she always did.

Turning away from her, Brie grinned with excite-ment. She could just imagine the smile on the woman's face when she opened the unexpected gifts.

There was a lightness in Brie's step as she continued her walk. Everything about the morning suddenly seemed more colorful and beautiful. Even the ocean waves sounded more enticing.

Now confident the old woman's canine companion would be getting the help it needed, her entire outlook on things changed.

The best part was knowing that Sir was waiting for her at the end of her walk. Taking a quick peek into the trashcan on her way back, Brie verified that the gift was gone and hurried home.

She was surprised to find the house was quiet when she entered, so she tiptoed to the bedroom to see if Sir had fallen back asleep. Instead, she found him lying on the bed, playing with himself.

Brie stood in the doorway, transfixed as she watched her Master stroke his rigid shaft in the natural light shining into the room.

Sir glanced up.

The power of his intense stare caused goosebumps to rise on her skin. He continued to stroke himself as he looked at her. His shaft was wet with precome, letting her know he was close to the edge.

"Come to me," he commanded in a low voice.

Brie's heart raced as she approached the bed. She fully expected Sir to order her to suck his cock, but he growled lustfully, "Strip."

With graceful movements, she slipped out of her clothes, then trembled with excitement as she waited for his next command.

"Lay beside me," he ordered, his voice hoarse with lust.

Climbing into bed beside Sir, she continued to watch as he stroked himself. It was a rare and incredibly intimate moment.

"Do you like watching?"

She glanced up at him, giving him a seductive smile. "I do, Sir."

Brie's heart skipped a beat when he took her hand and placed it on his shaft while he continued to stroke himself.

When she grasped his shaft tightly, matching his rhythm, she was delighted to see another bead of precome form on the tip of his shaft.

"I'm close," he groaned, stroking his cock slower.

Brie met his rhythm, excited at the idea of watching him come.

Instead, he abruptly stopped and ordered her to ride his shaft. "I need to feel that wet pussy."

Brie obediently straddled him, moaning in excitement as his hard shaft entered her pussy. Sir grabbed her hips and pushed himself deep inside of her.

"I love watching you fuck me," he growled.

Taking this position always had the hint of a power play to it. Just like sucking his cock, riding his shaft made her feel like she had power over him.

Knowing Sir was teetering on the edge, she decided to tease herself with his shaft, well aware that it would drive him wild. She grasped his cock and lifted herself so she could rub her wet pussy with the tip of his cock.

He groaned as she flicked her clit with just the head of his shaft.

"Naughty girl," he murmured huskily as he watched her use his cock to play with herself.

Sensing how turned-on he was, she pressed his cock

against her opening and slowly impaled herself onto his shaft. He threw his head back, letting out a tortured groan.

That masculine groan was music to her ears.

Brie ground herself against him, forcing his cock as deep as she could, then she slowly lifted herself.

Sir grabbed her hips again, watching intently as she sank back down on his cock. This time, he guided her movements as she moved up and down on his shaft.

He was very strategic, making sure the angle of his cock rubbed against her swollen G-spot as she rode him.

"Come with me," he commanded after several minutes. "I'll count down."

Her eyes widened, excited by the idea. Placing her hands on his chest for leverage, she prepared herself for the challenge.

"Are you ready, babygirl?"

"So, so ready."

His eyes flashed with intensity as he began slowly counting down. "Five...four..."

Brie kept her eyes on him and concentrated on the fullness of his shaft as he repeatedly rubbed her G-spot. Her nipples hardened realizing her Master was about to come inside her.

"Three...two..." he continued in that deep, gravelly voice that made her pussy ache with desire.

Then he paused for a moment.

Her entire body was on fire as she waited for permission to give in to her climax.

Sir's voice was strained when he finally called out, "...one."

Brie closed her eyes, moaning in pleasure when she felt him start to come inside her. His shaft pulsed with each release. That feeling sent her over the edge, her inner muscles contracting around his shaft as she joined him in orgasm.

She opened her eyes, finding it extremely erotic to gaze down into his eyes as they climaxed together.

Sir reached up to pull her down so he could feel her naked chest against his as the last pulses of their orgasms ended. Their connection was so intimate, she lay there in his arms, not wanting the moment to end.

Listening to his rapid heartbeat, Brie smiled. "Thank you for my reward, Sir. May I request an encore?"

His chest reverberated with a low chuckle. "You are a greedy thing."

She lifted her head and answered without shame. "I am, Sir."

Feeling nostalgic after Hope's recent birthday, Brie got out the basket of wedding gifts they'd received and laid them on the bed. Only weeks after their wedding, Sir had almost died in the plane crash and their lives stopped.

Looking through the cards reminded Brie of that joyous moment when they first had become man and wife—before the tragedy.

She'd had no idea then what was coming...

Feeling wistful, she sat down on the bed and opened the card from Sir's cousin Benito. Brie hadn't known him personally at the time, but he'd become very dear to her after their recent visit to Italy.

She chuckled when she remembered the long talk the two of them had as he drove her back from Gino's to meet Sir at the hospital just before Nonna's surgery. At the time, Benito had been so worried about Nonna that he couldn't stop drumming his fingers on the steering wheel. Brie had found it endearing.

Looking at his wedding card now, she couldn't have known how much he would mean to her.

Brie naturally gravitated to Tono's card next and picked it up. He had painted a flower on the front of the card. She ran her hand over it and felt his calming presence surround her. She opened the card, tears coming to her eyes when she read his words.

A solemn vow of support
Given to my chosen family

Tono honored that vow soon after writing it, rushing to Brie's side when Sir was fighting for his life. Despite having chosen Sir as her Master, their special bond remained unbreakable. Brie could not imagine her life without the Kinbaku Master in it. Kissing the card tenderly, she set Tono's card aside, wanting to frame it.

Brie chuckled as she picked up Master Anderson's card. It had a bare-chested photo of him holding Cayenne. Grinning, she opened the card to read what he had written.

What do you give the couple who has everything? A
date to weed with us in the buff!

Naturally, they'd never taken him up on that invitation, but Brie loved the photo and added it to the pile to be framed.

She grabbed the silver envelope next, having forgotten who'd given it to them. Inside were Marquis Gray's handwritten words:

The Gift of a Traditional Thai Cooking Class for Two

(Tomato and egg dishes are lacking)

She laughed. Marquis Gray had a rare sense of humor that few people knew existed because he was so intense.

Unfortunately, because of the crash, they never took the cooking course he had purchased for them. With a new baby on the way, she was unsure if they ever would.

"Such a shame…" she muttered as she set it down and selected another card.

The card was from Mr. Gallant.

Cash is customary but too impersonal for a couple
we both hold in high esteem
Our gift to the newlyweds
A jump off the Bridge to Nowhere
Enjoy

Brie tsked as she picked up the gift card for a bungee jump for two. Although the idea both scared and excited her, she knew there was no way would they be doing this anytime soon.

The next card happened to be Captain's present of a gift certificate for a hot air balloon ride for two. She shook her head, placing them in the growing pile of unused gifts.

"Another fun event we'll never experience…"

She reached out for the red envelope from Baron.

She opened it up and stared at the simple message.

An invitation to teach.

Reading those words stirred a longing inside her.

Sir had talked about doing lessons with Baron, but it had never worked out because life kept interrupting their plans.

But Sir deserved the opportunity to teach again.

Staring at the card, Brie promised herself that she would give him that chance.

"Your Master said I would find you here," the Russian growled, interrupting her thoughts. "But, this was not what I expected you'd be doing."

Brie giggled and patted the bed, inviting him to join her. "I'm just going through our wedding gifts. It feels like forever since we got married, even though it's only been a couple of years."

He chuckled somberly as he sat down. "I'm not surprised you feel that way, *radost moya*. A lot has happened since you became a bride."

Rytsar reached out and picked up the card he gave them, handing it to her.

Brie grinned as she opened it and read out loud:

The Isle

"At least this is one gift we have enjoyed on multiple occasions."

He smirked, leaning in closer to her. "I would like to make it an annual event."

"Oh, that would be fun…" she agreed, closing her eyes when his lips pressed against hers.

When the doorbell rang, Rytsar told her to ignore it

as he kissed her again.

Brie's eyes popped open when she heard Sir answer the door and her mother's voice filled the air.

"It's my parents!"

Rytsar looked as surprised as she did.

"Were you expecting them?"

She shook her head.

"Go greet your mother," Rytsar ordered, smacking her hard on the ass as she left the room.

"There you are!" her mother cried, running up to her.

Brie hugged her mom, then looked over her shoulder at her father. "Why the surprise visit? Is everything okay?"

"Everything is fine, little girl," her father assured her.

Brie went to hug him next. "So, what gives, Daddy?"

He smirked, glancing at her mother. "We just bought a house."

Brie looked at him questioningly, then turned to her mother. "Where?"

"Pasadena!" her mother squeaked.

Brie couldn't believe it. "You bought a house in California?"

"That we did, little girl."

Her mother gushed, "I couldn't stand missing Hope's birthday and all the other special things as she grows up."

Brie looked at Sir. "Did you know?"

He shook his head, smiling. "First I've heard of it."

"The best part is we can be your built-in babysitters from now on. Pasadena is only an hour away, so we can take care of Hope whenever you want." Her mother glanced around the room. "Where is my precious grandbaby, anyway?"

"She's been keeping me company in my office," Sir informed her. "Let me get her for you."

"Oh no, let me," her mom insisted.

Brie heard Hope start to cry when her mother entered the office. "This is exactly why we had to move," her mother lamented as she walked back out with Hope squirming in her arms. "She doesn't remember me."

Brie walked over and hugged her mom as she told Hope, "Look, Grandma and Grandpa are here!"

Hope held out her arms to Brie.

Once she was safe in Brie's arms, Hope quieted down and pointed at her mother. "That's right, sweet pea, that's your grandma."

Brie set Hope down on the floor and smiled as Hope toddled toward her.

"I can't believe she's walking already," her father said in awe. "I mean, you told us, but to see her walking with my own eyes…" He shook his head in disbelief. "Marcy was right. Life's too short to miss moments like this."

"What about all of your friends?" Brie asked in concern. "Won't it be hard to start over?"

Her mother picked Hope up and smiled. "We'll manage just fine."

Brie's father walked up to Rytsar and smacked him on the back. "Now you won't be saddled with the kid anymore. You're welcome."

Brie wondered how Rytsar felt about it, considering how much he loved their little girl—but she needn't have worried.

Rytsar smiled as he gazed down at Hope. "I never minded, Mr. Bennett. But knowing that *moye solntse* will be growing up with her grandparents nearby is reason to celebrate. Will you share a shot of vodka with me?"

"Don't mind if I do," he answered, smacking Rytsar on the back again.

Brie glanced at Rytsar and smiled.

He was right. Having her mom and dad become an integral part of their children's lives was an unexpected and priceless gift.

Later that night when they retired to the bedroom, Sir noticed the wedding cards still scattered on the bed. He picked up one and smirked. "So, this was what you were up to in the bedroom."

Brie started quickly gathering them up, having forgotten about them after the excitement of the day. "I was feeling a bit nostalgic, Sir."

Noticing the two separate piles, he asked, "What were you doing with them?"

She picked up the smaller stack. "I was going to frame these to hang them up."

"And these?" he asked, picking up the other pile.

She looked at him sadly. "Those are all the gifts we never used."

He glanced through them with a thoughtful look, before handing them to her. "It seems like a lifetime ago."

"I guess it was, really."

He nodded and was silent. She could see the pain in his eyes as he relived the plane crash.

"Sir," she said gently. "I was wondering. Do you think Marquis Gray would mind if I gave his gift to my parents instead? Knowing how solitary my dad is, it would give them both a way to get out in their new community."

"There's no harm in asking, babygirl."

With Sir's permission, Brie contacted Marquis Gray the next day and explained what she wanted to do with the cooking course and why.

Marquis did not hesitate in his answer. "It would be an excellent use of the certificate."

"Thank you for the thoughtful gift. I'm sorry we never had the chance to enjoy it ourselves."

"Life is full of unexpected challenges, Mrs. Davis. There's no need to apologize. I'm happy to hear it will be put to good use." He paused for a moment and asked, "How are you doing?"

The concern in his voice touched Brie. "I am well, Marquis."

"Has a decision been made on how to proceed with Lilly?"

"Not yet. You've given Sir a lot to consider."

"I'm glad to hear he is thinking it through before taking action. I was certain he would. Take care, Mrs. Davis, and give your Master my best."

Brie was comforted by his words, secure in the knowledge that the rift between the two men had not damaged their friendship.

Returning Home

Soon after her parents officially moved into their new house, Brie and Sir went to visit them with Hope in tow.

Brie handed Marquis's gift to her mother. "Happy housewarming!"

Her mother opened the envelope and smiled, showing it to Brie's dad. "That sounds like so much fun!"

Her father huffed. "I don't cook, Brianna. You know that."

Brie grinned, figuring he would say that. "You can just observe, Daddy. Nothing says you have to participate in the cooking sessions. I just thought it would be nice for you two to get out and meet people. It comes highly recommended by Marquis Gray."

"Oh, really?" He suddenly looked interested.

Brie knew how much her father respected the Dom and wasn't surprised when he muttered, "I suppose I could go just to support your mom."

Her mom threw her arms around him. "Thank you, honey!"

Brie's dad rolled his eyes but followed it up by giving

her a quick peck on the cheek.

For all his complaining, her dad really did have a soft heart.

"Now for the whole reason we moved to La La Land in the first place. Come here, cutie," her father said, taking Hope from her arms. "Grandpa's got a whole lot of spoiling to catch up on."

Sir spoke up. "We appreciate you taking Hope for the night."

"Anytime, Thane," her mother said, giggling. "This feels like a dream, being able to see you throughout the year and getting to babysit Hope to our hearts' content."

"It's a blessing to us as well, Mom," Brie told her, squeezing Sir's hand.

Her father stared at them for a moment, then shook his head. "I don't want to know where you are going or what you will be doing." He raised his hand. "As far as I'm concerned, you don't exist beyond these walls. It's the only way I can keep my sanity."

"Daddy!" Brie cried.

"Just telling you like it is, little girl. Now off you go. Your mother and I have a lot of time to make up with our granddaughter."

It was humorous to Brie. After being the center of her parents' universe her whole life, her parents now cared more about being with Hope than with her. As Brie walked to the car with Sir, she laughed. "I don't think they would complain if we never came back."

Sir smirked as he opened the passenger door and helped her into the car. "I plan to take full advantage of their generous offer."

"Where are we going, Sir?"

He glanced at her, a wicked glint in his eye. "I have

one of the top graduates of the Submissive Training Center, and I believe it's time to give her a challenge worthy of her talent."

Brie suddenly felt tingles of excitement.

"Eyes forward, téa, hands in your lap, and no questions," he commanded.

Brie's heart began to race as she sat still, being his obedient sub, while her imagination went crazy. She wondered what he had planned.

She was shocked when they pulled into the full parking lot of the college that housed the Submissive Training Center.

Brie knew the Submissive Training course was in session and turned to ask Sir about it.

He tsked in disapproval.

She blanched, immediately realized what she'd done, and cried out, "I'm sorry, Master!"

"What did you do wrong, téa?"

"I failed to look forward."

He nodded. "As your Master, it is my duty to punish you for disobeying me."

It had been a while since Brie had been formally punished. "Yes, Master."

"While you wait for your punishment, see that you don't disobey me again."

"I won't, Master," she promised. Instead of feeling shame, Brie felt exhilarated. Not because she'd been disobedient—that was regrettable—but because she'd enjoyed being challenged again.

"The stress of Lilly, along with the pressures of Holloway's attack on your career and the demands of my work, have made it easy for me to become complacent as your Master. We cannot allow that to happen, now can we, téa?"

Brie shook her head vigorously while staring forward. "No, Master."

"Your parents' move to California allows me the opportunity to provide you with more formal encounters. Something I know we both desire."

Brie felt the butterflies start. "I love that idea, Master."

He placed his finger under her chin and turned her head to gaze into her eyes. "Are you ready to please your Master, téa?"

"Yes..." she murmured breathlessly as he leaned in and claimed her lips. His possessive kiss left her whole body trembling afterward.

Sir reached behind his seat and took out a red case. Brie noticed it wasn't the tool bag he normally carried. He got out of the car and walked around to the passenger side, opening the door for her.

As Sir helped her out of the vehicle, Brie was overcome with giddiness remembering how it felt to be a student here.

In a cool, commanding voice he said simply, "Follow."

Brie obediently walked behind her Master, her entire body tingling with excitement.

Walking through the entrance of the college took Brie back to that first day and she let out a sigh of elation.

"Good evening, Sir Davis," Rachael replied from the receptionist's desk. She used the formal tone she reserved for the staff at the Center. Brie kept her eyes lowered, focused exclusively on Sir.

The college itself was full of business students busily

making their way to their evening classes but Sir headed directly to the elevator. When the doors opened, she stood proudly beside her Master in silent anticipation.

Upon leaving the elevator, Brie recognized the familiar voice of Mr. Gallant behind the closed classroom door. Master Anderson, who was now the Headmaster of the school, was walking down the hallway. He was involved in an intense conversation with Mistress Lou, one of the other trainers.

Master Anderson looked up for a moment and nodded to Sir before continuing his discussion with the Mistress.

Being here tonight was like having a backstage pass to the inner workings of the Submissive Training Center as an outside observer. Brie smiled to herself as she followed Sir down the hallway, thinking how nervous and excited the submissives currently taking the course must be.

Lucky...

However, they were not as lucky as Brie, who was not only collared to the former Headmaster but was about to enjoy a new challenge from the handsome Dom.

Sir stopped in front of the restrooms and handed her the red case he'd been carrying. "This is an updated version of your uniform. Change and meet me at Room 158."

Brie took it from him with reverence and walked into the room to change. This particular restroom had an area sectioned off for changing and was equipped with lockers and a full-length mirror.

She set the case on the counter and opened it, excited to see what Sir had picked out for her. Brie looked at the pieces and smiled to herself. The outfit was similar in style to her old uniform, but instead of being made of brown leather, the corset was black with red laces and had a matching flared skirt with an elastic band that could expand as her belly grew. Rather than crotchless pantyhose, her legs were bare as she donned the red thong and slipped into a pair of sexy strapless heels. She was grateful Sir had considered the months ahead by selecting heels that were *not* six-inches high.

Brie stood in front of the mirror, biting her lip. Not only did wearing this uniform instantly transform her mindset into that of a student, but Sir had great taste in clothing. She felt incredibly sexy wearing it.

Walking out of the restroom, Brie headed to the far end of the school where the Dominants Training Center held classes. She smiled to herself as she listened to the satisfying sound of her heels clicking down the hallway.

Sir was waiting for her outside Room 158. He was holding a blindfold. The lust in his eyes as he looked her up and down made her tremble in expectation.

"Turn and face away from me."

Brie dutifully turned, smiling to herself as he placed the red blindfold over her eyes and adjusted it.

"Can you see?" he asked once it was secured.

"No, Master."

"Good."

He opened the door and led her into the room, guiding her to the center. "Kneel."

Brie gracefully knelt on the floor and waited for his next command.

"Do not move or make a sound until I return."

She listened to his retreating footsteps as he left the room and wondered how long he would make her wait.

That's when she heard someone move beside her and realized she was not alone. Not knowing who it was or what was about to happen had Brie quivering with excitement.

"Brie? Is that you?"

She couldn't believe who it was and fought hard not to smile. She wanted desperately to answer her friend but felt certain Sir would be observing her through one of the hidden cameras in the room.

"I know it's you. I totally recognized Sir's voice," Lea whispered.

Brie continued to remain silent, although not answering Lea was killing her.

In the barest of whispers, Lea said, "Hey, Bennett, you know you are a submissive when you wish your MasterCard would give you orders."

Brie's lips trembled in her effort to keep from smiling. She couldn't believe Lea was telling her the same joke she had the night they became friends at the Center. Was she seriously trying to get both of them in trouble—again?

Memories of those six weeks of class flooded Brie's mind and all she wanted was to hug her best friend. Still, she was determined to please Sir and did not move.

After several minutes, Lea murmured, "Wow. You're a tough cookie, Stinky Cheese. I can see why you were the top of our class."

Brie had to fight off another giggle and silently vowed to make her friend pay in the future.

When Sir finally walked back into the room, Brie distinctly heard another man's footsteps and was instantly on alert.

"You have done well, téa," Sir complimented her,

taking off the blindfold.

Brie gazed up into his eyes, falling in love with him all over again.

"Unfortunately, the same cannot be said of my sub." Brie instantly recognized Hunter's commanding tone. "I'm afraid she will have to be punished."

Lea let out a little squeak.

"Téa is still awaiting a punishment she earned on the way here."

Brie blushed but took heart, knowing she would be sharing her punishment with Lea.

"How would you like me to proceed, Sir Davis?" Hunter asked him.

"It was a small infraction. Exercise your own discretion."

Brie's stomach did a flip-flop. Sir was going to allow Hunter to scene with her?

"As you witnessed for yourself, sprite was exceedingly disobedient."

Brie heard her friend gasp and felt sympathy for her. However, Brie was charmed after hearing Hunter's pet name for Lea was "sprite".

It totally fit her girlfriend.

"I will adjust her punishment accordingly," Sir replied gravely.

Lea let out a soft whimper.

Her poor friend probably thought she was going to play out a brat scene with Hunter, and now she would have to face punishment from the Headmaster who helped train her.

"Shall we meet up in say…an hour?" Sir asked.

Hunter glanced at Brie and nodded. "An hour would work well."

"Excellent."

Turning to Lea, Sir stated, "Come with me, Ms. Taylor."

Brie was unsure what Sir would do but was certain he would be fair in his punishment. How embarrassing for Lea to be punished by the former Headmaster when she was a successful graduate of the school—especially when it was the same infraction she had been punished for as a trainee.

It was hard for Brie not to giggle.

After they left the room and the door closed, Brie felt the nerves kick in.

She was alone with a new Dom.

"I believe in swift punishment," Hunter stated.

Brie swallowed hard and nodded.

"Stand and lean against the bench," he ordered in a voice that commanded respect.

Taking a deep breath, Brie stood up gracefully and moved to the bench.

She heard him searching through the cabinet of tools behind her before saying, "Ah, this should do nicely."

Brie stiffened as she heard him walk back to her.

"Why are you being punished?" Hunter asked.

"I failed to keep my eyes facing forward."

"Then one strike should suffice. Lift your skirt."

Brie closed her eyes, trying to stay calm as she slowly lifted the material of her skirt. She knew Hunter had graduated at the top of his class and Lea spoke highly of him, but she still felt a twinge of fear. She wondered what tool he was about to use for her punishment. Would it be a crop, a belt, or possibly a cane?

Brie forced herself to remain still as she waited.

"Make no sound," Hunter ordered.

Chills coursed down her spine as he placed his hand on her back.

When the strike came, the hard smack of the wooden paddle took her breath away. The impact reverberated through her body. Tears pricked her eyes and it took everything in her not to yelp.

Hunter set the paddle down and readjusted her skirt before turning her around to face him.

He looked her in the eyes when he told her, "You are forgiven."

Brie could not express the power those words had over her. Even though her infraction had been slight and the punishment easy, relief flooded through her. Having it completely absolved pleased her submissive soul.

"Thank you."

He nodded in acknowledgment, then commanded, "Bow to me."

There was something in Hunter's tone that made her insides quiver. She remembered having the same feeling when she'd scened with him on Kinky Eve.

She felt a driving and instinctual urge to bow at his feet and did so immediately.

"Do you submit to me for this scene?"

Brie felt goosebumps rise on her skin as she experienced a feeling of déjà vu. It was as if she was returning to those first days at the Training Center, back when she'd been asked to submit to Doms she hadn't known personally.

It filled her with a sense of fearful excitement.

"Yes," she replied confidently, but she trembled slightly knowing she had just consented to scene with him for the next hour.

"You may stand and face your Master."

Brie stood before him, curious about what he had planned.

"Sir Davis tells me you enjoy bondage."

"I do…" She hesitated for a moment, not knowing how to address him. "What should I call you?"

He raised an eyebrow. "Master, of course."

She felt butterflies in her stomach. It was a challenge for her because it was the same title Sir used whenever they formally scened together. Although the title was common, for Brie it required another level of submission. She suspected Hunter knew that by the way he was staring at her expectantly.

Well, she'd come tonight to be challenged, so she answered firmly, "Yes, Master."

"I will call you naiad. Do you know what that is?"

Brie shook her head.

"Water nymphs, which are said to inhabit rivers, springs, and waterfalls. They're beautiful and lighthearted but can be dangerous to mortals."

Again, she was charmed by his choice of a pet name and bowed to him. "I'm honored to be called such a name."

He inclined his head with a slight smile on his lips. "Remove your clothes except for your panties, then turn away from me. Common safewords apply, but it's up to you to use them."

Brie understood two things without Hunter having to explain. "Green," "yellow," and "red" were her safewords, but he would not be checking on her because he expected her to call them out if necessary.

Taking a deep breath, Brie centered herself before the scene. She removed her corset and skirt with poised, unhurried movements, laying them in a neat pile on the floor beside her shoes.

She then turned away from him and waited with bated breath.

Hunter approached her and she felt his fingers lightly following the curve of her shoulders. His hands were deceptively gentle which helped ease her nerves.

"Mount the platform and kneel in an open position," he commanded, pointing to a large cube that stood three feet off the ground.

Brie climbed onto it and knelt with her hands at her sides, open and relaxed. She kept her legs closed and her back straight.

"Open your thighs."

Brie adjusted her position. The new pose made her feel more exposed, heightening her sense of vulnerability.

Hunter grazed his finger along her cheekbone and jawline. "You have good genetics, naiad, every feature designed to entice."

Studying her intently, he walked around the platform slowly. Hunter reached out to touch her hair. "The female body was built for pleasure. I've spent many years unlocking its secrets and have discovered some which you may be unaware of."

Brie felt a pleasant tension between them. He was confident in his dominance which called to her submissive spirit.

"There are times when a little pain can enhance pleasure—even when you are not a masochist. Wouldn't you agree?"

Brie's nervousness returned. "Yes, Master."

She felt a surge of excitement when he produced a length of nylon rope.

Hunter was gentle but firm when he grabbed her wrists and bound them behind her back. Holding her elbows together, he forced her shoulders back making her back arch which pushed out her breasts.

Wrapping the rope around her elbows, he gave a tug, forcing them to touch. He then began the slow process of binding her forearms together.

This was an extremely demanding pose. Brie had seen riggers use it at various dungeons, but she had never experienced it for herself. The binding forced Brie to mentally submit to the challenge of the pose or be overwhelmed by the physical demands of it.

Hunter took his time as he tied each knot, compelling Brie to submit to the rope—and his will.

When he finished tying the final one, he stood back to admire his work and then walked around her. "You are a feast for the eyes, naiad."

She basked in his praise but felt a twinge of apprehension when he walked back to the cabinet to grab more items.

"Bound as you are, your breasts are completely at my mercy."

Brie's heart quickened.

To her relief, he began by grazing her nipples with a feather tickler. The sensation was extremely pleasant. Just as she had been taught during training, Brie voiced her pleasure to her Dom by moaning softly.

Hunter focused the stimulation solely on her breasts, circling them with the toy before returning to tickle her hard nipples. The light sensation caused goosebumps to rise on her skin.

"Do you believe I can make you come through nipple play alone?"

Brie was inspired by the look of confidence in his eyes and nodded.

Hunter put down the feather tool and picked up a small flogger. He began flicking the rubber instrument across her breasts. The sound of the tails slapping against her skin was sensually exciting to hear, but it was the way he skillfully used the tool that held Brie's attention.

Hunter wasn't using the flogger as a way to torture her breasts but to stimulate them. Each strike of the small flogger was sexually stimulating, like the caress of a rough but dedicated lover. Brie's body responded eagerly to his attention.

Tied as she was, Brie was completely focused on what he was doing. A surge of heat traveled from the nipple he was teasing straight down to her pussy. She moaned louder and felt her thong getting wet.

Hunter increased the intensity of each strike without increasing the pain, the rhythmic contact emulating the bounce of her breasts while being taken forcefully.

Brie lost herself in the sensation but then whimpered when he stopped. She was reluctant for the pleasure to end.

That's when he picked up a small, dark vibrator with a red tip. He turned it on, and she listened as he adjusted the pulse and intensity of it.

"Naiad, close your eyes and concentrate on the vibration."

Brie immediately shut her eyes and answered dutifully, "Yes, Master."

He brought the toy to her breast but did not make contact, letting the sound of its vibration tease her. When he finally pressed it against the sensitive skin of her areola, she felt pleasant electrical sparks radiate from her nipple down to her pussy. When he moved to her other breast, the sensation only increased.

"Submit to me."

His words released the sexual tension that had been building in her body. Rather than fight against it, Brie embraced the powerful climax threatening to overtake her.

Her body started shuddering uncontrollably. The strength of the orgasm was restrained by the limits of his rope and Brie let out a long desperate cry as it rocked through her.

Hunter wrapped an arm around her to support her. He continued to graze her nipples with the small vibrator, making the orgasm linger—the vibration from the toy complementing the pulses of her release.

"Good girl," he said with satisfaction as the last of her climax ebbed away.

Brie was spent after it ended and leaned against him, still trembling from the powerful orgasm.

Hunter gently laid her on her side and began the process of untying the rope. When the last knot was untied and she was free from the tight constraint of the rope, Brie experienced a wave of euphoria.

He joined her on the platform and laid her head against him as he embraced her in silence, letting her come down slowly.

Brie lay against him, her heart still racing, enjoying the afterglow of the scene.

When Sir arrived with Lea a short time later, Brie

looked at him with a slow smile.

"I see the session went well," he complimented with a gleam in his eyes.

"She is a pleasure to scene with, Sir Davis."

He presented Lea to Hunter. "Your charge is ready for further instruction."

Brie turned her head slowly and saw that Lea's eyes were glued on Hunter. Her insatiable need for him was a palpable force in the room.

"Thank you, Sir Davis." As Hunter slowly disengaged himself from Brie, he told him, "I will leave you to finish with aftercare."

Standing up, Hunter faced Lea. "Come, sprite. I have a deep and penetrating lesson waiting for you."

Lea whimpered in delight, smiling at Brie on the way out.

Once they were alone, Sir joined Brie on the platform, enclosing her in his protective embrace. He kissed her on the lips and asked, "Did you enjoy the challenge, téa?"

She gazed up into his beautiful eyes. "Very much, Master."

"I felt tonight would both challenge and excite you."

"You are right...on both counts." She lifted her chin, silently begging for another kiss.

Sir slipped his hand between her legs as he pressed his lips firmly against hers. "Your Master longs to feel the depth of your excitement."

Brie smiled as she opened her legs to him, moaning hungrily when he ripped off her wet thong.

"You are so wet, téa." He bit her neck as he slipped his finger inside her.

Tingling chills overtook her when Sir repositioned

himself between her legs. He stared down at her as he pressed the head of his cock against her opening. "Prepare to be claimed."

Brie looked up at him, her body aching for him. "Please…"

His eyes flashed with a dangerous glint as he took her wrists in one hand, forcing them above her head as he thrust his cock into her.

The night had heightened Brie's need for him, the familiar setting reinforcing the dynamic they shared.

Without reservation, Brie gave in fully to his unbridled passion, crying out in ecstasy as he ramped up his thrusts and claimed his collared submissive.

It was like returning home…

Afterward, as they lay panting together on the platform, Sir asked her, "Tell me your thoughts about tonight."

Brie grinned. "I was surprised by Lea."

He chuckled lightly. "I thought you might enjoy that."

She looked up at the ceiling. "I was also surprised you left me alone with Hunter."

Sir brushed away an errant strand of hair from her face. "I knew if I stayed in the room, your thoughts would have gravitated toward me and not remained on the scene."

Brie nodded, realizing that he was right.

"What did you learn tonight, téa?" he asked in a more serious tone.

She gave it careful consideration before answering. "My deepest desire as a submissive…" She paused, looking deep into his eyes. "…is to never stop learning."

He nodded, satisfied with her answer. "Yes. It makes

you a particularly challenging sub."

She smiled apologetically.

Grazing his thumb against her cheek, he told her, "I wouldn't have it any other way."

Blessed Event

B rie set out on her usual morning walk, cherishing the alone time to reflect on things while taking in the beauty of the ocean. Almost six months into the pregnancy, she was definitely showing, but she could still walk without a waddle.

She wasn't looking forward to that part of her pregnancy, because it would also usher in the period of no sleep because of the baby kicking her at all hours of the night. Hope had been an active baby that last trimester and Brie expected no less from this little one.

Brie looked up to see the old woman rummaging for plastic bottles in the trashcan and smiled. Her plan to help the little dog had been a success. It turned out the poor pup was suffering from a severe case of mange that could have proven deadly if left untreated. Thankfully, with medical attention, he'd recovered and his fur was now growing back.

She waved at the old woman, who huffed before bending down to dig for more bottles. Brie noticed the woman only wore the pretty socks she'd given her, so she had followed it up by anonymously leaving a new pair every month—just before the older socks wore out.

Although the woman's demeanor hadn't changed, she no longer had that worried look in her eyes. She could go about her day providing for them both without the heavy burden of her companion's health weighing her down.

The knowledge that she'd come up with a way to help the woman without making her feel uncomfortable brought joy to Brie's heart. And, getting to pick out new socks with Hope every month kept the joy of it going.

In a world where it was easy to feel alone and invisible, Brie was grateful she'd been able to let this woman know someone saw her and cared.

Kylie called Brie unexpectedly, begging Brie to come to the hospital.

"What's wrong?"

"I'm in labor, but the baby wasn't supposed to come for two more weeks!"

Brie remembered how terrified she'd been when she was rushed to the hospital weeks before Hope was due. "It's going to be okay," she assured Kylie. "I had Hope three weeks early and everything worked out. Dr. Glas is amazing."

"Yes, he is," she agreed, then whimpered, "But, I'm nervous."

"Faelan will be with you the entire time. I remember what a huge comfort it was having Sir by my side when Hope was born."

Kylie was silent for several moments before replying.

"It's just that I have this feeling…"

Brie chuckled lightly. "It's completely normal to feel anxious your first time. I felt the exact same way with Hope."

"That's right! You even had complications during delivery."

"I did, but Hope is okay. Dr. Glas has lots of experience delivering babies. Trust me. You're in excellent hands."

Kylie let out an uneasy sigh. "Because I'm early, neither of our parents can get here before tomorrow. Brie…it would mean a lot to me if you were here."

Brie didn't even think twice after hearing the fear in Kylie's voice. "Of course. I'll be there as soon as I can." She wrote down the address for the hospital.

After hanging up, Brie informed Sir about what was going on. He surprised her by insisting on driving her there himself.

"What about Hope?"

"I'm certain Rytsar will watch her," he answered, grabbing his keys.

Touched by his kind gesture, Brie felt the need to warn him. "You know the delivery could take hours, Sir. We may end up staying there overnight."

He smirked with amusement. "I'm well aware. However, considering the baby is two weeks early and they'll be concerned, it's important to have family there."

His answer melted Brie's heart. Even though there had once been a strong rivalry between Faelan and Sir, their relationship had changed drastically since. She smiled, telling him, "I know it will mean a lot to them both."

He nodded curtly, scooping Hope up in his arms.

They made the short drive to Rytsar's place. While he was getting Hope out of the car seat, Brie bounded up to the porch and rang the doorbell. She was surprised when Maxim swung the door open and she saw a bunch of men chatting loudly in Russian.

"Oh, I'm sorry," she sputtered. "I didn't realize Rytsar had company."

"*Radost moya!*" she heard from deep within the house. Rytsar made his way through the crowd to greet her personally. "What brings you here?"

Just as she was about to answer, Sir came walking up behind her with Hope in his arms.

"*Moye solntse.*" Rytsar grinned as he grabbed Hope from him. Turning around to face the men, he announced, "This is the child I've been speaking about."

All the men all stared at the baby solemnly.

Turning around, Rytsar asked Sir, "What do you need, comrade?"

"We were going to ask you to watch her."

Rytsar suddenly frowned. "What's wrong, *moy droog?*"

Sir lowered his voice. "Kylie has been rushed to the hospital because of the baby and asked for Brie to join her. I thought Faelan might appreciate some company as well."

The Russian's eyes flashed with pain as he looked down at Hope. "I remember the fear I suffered during this babe's delivery. I would not wish that on the Wolf Pup."

Rytsar turned to face his guests. "Gentlemen, unfortunately, I must ask you to leave. We will continue this discussion tomorrow."

"There's no nee—" Brie sputtered.

Rytsar held his hand up to stop her. "*Moye solntse* is

safe with me. Go comfort your friend."

Brie handed Titov the diaper bag and smiled at Rytsar with tears in her eyes, mouthing the words, *Thank you.*

As soon as Sir pulled out of the driveway, he hit the gas. Brie was thrown against the back of the seat as the car took off. Skilled behind the wheel, Sir got them to the hospital safely and in record time. Pulling up to the entrance, he told her, "I'll park the car. You find out the room number and text me. I'll join you as soon as I can."

Brie gave him a quick peck on the cheek before getting out of the car. She walked into the hospital, heading straight to the front desk. After getting Kylie's room number, she texted Sir and walked to the elevator.

An unsettling feeling washed over her as she waited for the elevator, so she decided to skip the elevator and take the stairs instead. Running up them, she burst onto the third floor, attracting the attention of the staff at the nurses' station.

One of them stood up, asking with concern, "May I help you?"

Brie panted. "I'm here to see Kylie. She asked me to come."

"Do you mean Mrs. Wallace?"

Brie's eyes widened.

Did Faelan and Kylie secretly get married?

The idea of it was incredibly romantic.

"Yes, Kylie Wallace. I'm her friend, Brianna Davis."

The nurse nodded. "I'll let her know you're here."

A few minutes later, Faelan came walking down the hallway to greet her. "Thanks for coming so quickly. Kylie isn't doing well."

Fear gripped Brie's heart. "What's going on?"

He shook his head. "Other than our little boy coming earlier than expected, everything seems to be going well. But Kylie can't shake the feeling that something's wrong."

Brie was relieved to hear the baby was okay and smiled. "I remember how terrified I felt with Hope, so I understand what she is going through. Everything is going to be okay."

"That's what I've been trying to tell her." He placed his hand on her shoulder. "Let's hope she'll listen to you."

Faelan led her down the corridor to the hospital room and forced a relaxed smile when he entered. "Look what I brought. Your favorite food."

"Brie!" Kylie cried.

Brie nudged Faelan in the ribs before walking to Kylie's bed. "I hear the baby is doing well."

Kylie nodded, sighing nervously. "That's what they keep telling me."

She took her friend's hand and squeezed it. "I'm honored you asked me to come. After having Hope, it made me really want to see a birth myself. Thank you."

"No, thank you!" The worried look in Kylie's eyes momentarily disappeared. "I feel so much better now that you're here."

Glancing at Faelan, Kylie added, "Not that you aren't enough, my love."

He walked to the other side of the bed to take her hand. "You are about to give birth to my child. There is nothing you could say to offend me."

Her eyes twinkled mischievously. "That almost sounds like a challenge."

Brie's phone suddenly pinged. She glanced down to read her text and told them, "It looks like Sir made it to the waiting room."

Faelan looked at Brie in surprise. "He came?"

"Sir insisted."

He seemed touched and replied, "I better go and say hello." Then he immediately turned to Kylie, adding, "Unless you need me to stay, of course."

Kylie laughed. "You can go now that Brie's here, and please thank Sir Davis for me."

"I certainly will, my wife." Leaning down, Faelan kissed her on the forehead. "Don't have too much fun without me."

After he left, Brie turned to Kylie. "Did I hear right? Did Faelan just call you 'wife?'"

Kylie blushed. "It's true. Although we originally planned to get married in a couple of years, this little one changed things." She rubbed her large belly. "Faelan thought it would be best to elope because it's important to him that the baby has his name and knows he was born out of love."

"Congratulations, Kylie!"

"Thanks," she said, beaming.

"What a romantic thing to do, but was it hard for you to give up a formal wedding?"

Her eyes twinkled. "Not at all. It wouldn't have mattered where we said 'I do.'"

Brie smiled. "You two really are perfect together."

Kylie looked down at her pregnant belly lovingly. "And soon it will be the three of us…" She shook her head with a bemused look on her face. "He even sold his beloved Mustang and bought a family-friendly SUV."

Brie smiled, truly shocked. "Wow! He's really taking this dad thing seriously."

"He really is." She grinned, looking up at Brie. "It was kind of Sir Davis to come with you. Faelan is trying hard to hide it but I can tell he's not handling this well, either."

Brie smiled at her. "It's obvious how much he cares about you."

There was a curt knock on the door.

Dr. Glas peeked in. "Just your friendly obstetrician, come to check your progress, lass."

Kylie giggled nervously and looked to Brie. "Dr. Glas, you know my friend Brie."

He smiled warmly. "Ah, yes. My patient who is not a masochist."

Brie's face burned with heat. She'd never forget screaming out those words while in the throes of labor. She struggled to keep a straight face when she answered him, "It remains true to this day."

His chuckle filled the room as he held out his hand to her, shaking it formally. "It's always a pleasure to see you, Mrs. Davis." He glanced down at her stomach. "And, I'll be seeing you and the next wee one for another checkup soon."

"You certainly will."

He turned his attention to Kylie. "But right now, it's all about you, Mrs. Wallace. How are you feeling?"

"Really nervous," she confessed.

"There's no reason to be," he assured her as he scrubbed his hands. Holding up his arms, he grinned. "You're in good hands with me."

A reluctant smile broke over Kylie's face.

"So, let's see how much you've progressed, shall we?" He slipped on a pair of gloves and settled between her legs. Keeping her discreetly covered, he manually checked her cervix. "We're at a good eight centimeters. It shouldn't be long now."

Kylie nodded, but there was no hiding the fear that was still present in her eyes.

Brie squeezed her hand. "You're going to do great." Watching the steady heartbeat on the baby's monitor, she added, "And your little guy isn't in any distress. That's a good sign."

"You promise to stay with me the whole time?" Kylie begged her.

"I won't leave your side, Brie promised. "I wouldn't miss this for the world."

Tears of gratitude filled Kylie's eyes. "Thank you, Brie. I don't know what I would do without your moral support right now…along with the epidural."

Brie chuckled. "I *am* jealous of you for that."

"Who knows, Mrs. Davis? If all goes well, you may get the chance to experience one yourself with this next birth." Dr. Glas winked at her as he pulled the gloves off.

"As for you, Mrs. Wallace, you're in the final stretch. Before long, you'll be holding your wee babe in your arms."

"I can't wait," Kylie murmured, still looking worried.

As Dr. Glas was leaving, Faelan returned with a confident grin on his face. It was obvious his talk with Sir had eased his apprehension. "How are you feeling?"

"Much better now that you're back," Kylie admitted, her relief easy to read. "Dr. Glas said it could be anytime now."

Faelan shook his head in amazement as he placed his hand on her stomach. "It's hard to believe we're about to meet the little tyke after waiting so long for this moment."

He glanced at Brie. "It doesn't seem real."

She smiled, understanding. "Nothing can prepare you for it." Looking down at her own belly, she added, "I feel the same way about this one."

"I'm so glad our kids will grow up together." Kylie squeezed her hand.

"We are going to have our hands full on play dates," Brie laughed. "Between Hope, Jonathan, and our two kiddos, we'll have a full gang."

Brie looked at Faelan. "Have you decided on a name yet?"

He glanced at Kylie, answering proudly, "We have."

"Faelan and I wanted to honor our fathers," Kylie explained. "So, we've chosen Luke Christian Wallace."

"I love that name!" Brie gushed, looking at the two of them.

"I'm grateful Kylie and I were born into strong families," Faelan told her. "And we plan to pass that on to our son."

Brie suddenly noticed Kylie's grimace. "A tough contraction?"

Kylie placed her hands on her stomach. "It doesn't hurt exactly. It's just uncomfortable. But, boy, they make my stomach hard as a rock."

"Just look at that spike," Faelan exclaimed, staring at the monitor. "Your body is getting serious about having this baby."

Brie stated at Kylie in disbelief. "You really aren't in

any pain right now?"

She smiled, nodding.

Brie laughed. "I'm pretty sure I was screaming my head off at this point."

Faelan's voice was full of pride. "You're doing great, baby!"

Kylie gazed up at him and begged, "Please kiss me."

Without hesitation, he leaned down and planted a passionate kiss on her lips. When he pulled away, she sighed in contentment. "I really needed that."

"Anytime, little wife."

Brie loved hearing Faelan call Kylie that and asked, "So, what was the wedding like?"

He chuckled. "It was quick and to the point. We toyed with the idea of having a formal wedding after the birth." He glanced at Kylie. "But it seemed silly to wait when we love each other."

"You can always throw a big reception when you're ready," Brie suggested. "I know all of us would enjoy the chance to celebrate with you two."

Faelan played with a lock of Kylie's hair. "We'll keep that in mind."

Kylie grimaced again. "Ugh…this one is a lot stronger."

Seeing the large spike, Faelan announced, "I'm getting Dr. Glas."

"I'm sure it's not necessary," Kylie told him.

"I'll feel better if I do."

Brie joked, "And, we know it's all about you."

Faelan winked at her before heading out the door.

Looking back at Kylie, she asked, "How are you feeling?"

"Excited…and terrified."

"That feeling still hasn't left yet?"

Kylie shook her head. "I know everything is going to be fine." She glanced at the monitor. "Just look how strong his heartbeat is."

Dr. Glas entered the room with Faelan right behind him. "Your husband seems to think you're about to deliver."

Kylie blushed. "I told him not to bother you."

"Let me check to determine if he is right."

Brie noticed a slow smile on his lips as he felt inside her. "I have to say, your husband's fathering instincts are impeccable. You are fully dilated, Mrs. Wallace."

Kylie's eyes widened, but Brie couldn't tell if it was out of relief or terror. "What happens now?"

"I call the nurse in and we deliver this wee one. If you feel the urge to push, I want you to breathe through it. I can't have you pushing quite yet."

She nodded vigorously. "I promise not to push until you give the command."

While they were waiting for the doctor to return, Brie hugged Kylie. "Your little boy is healthy and strong just like his mother."

Faelan looked tenderly at his wife. "You are an extraordinary woman."

"I don't feel like that right now." She panted heavily as she breathed through a contraction.

He leaned down and kissed her again once it was over. "But, you are."

Brie watched as Kylie's look of fear transformed into one of confidence as she breathed through another powerful contraction.

When Dr. Glas returned with the nurse, he started barking out orders. "Mr. Wallace, take your wife's left leg and lift it, cupping her heel for support."

When Brie saw Faelan hesitate, she walked over to Kylie's right side and lifted her leg the way Sir and Rytsar had done for her when she was delivering Hope.

Faelan immediately followed her example and chuckled at Kylie. "You'll have to forgive me. I'm new at this."

"Me, too," she laughed nervously.

The nurse explained, "They'll support you by making your pushes more effective."

Kylie nodded.

Dr, Glas settled between her legs and said in his adorable Scottish accent, "Now, we are going to work with your contractions, lass. When you feel one coming, I want you to push as long and hard as you can."

"You got it," Kylie answered.

When the next contraction came, Dr. Glas ordered, "Push, push, push!"

Kylie snarled like a fierce lioness as she braced against Brie and Faelan and began pushing hard.

When it passed she lay back, panting heavily.

"That was very good. This next one, don't stop until I say so."

Kylie was about to answer when the next contraction hit. Closing her eyes, her face turned a deep red as she pushed for all she was worth. Brie glanced down, excited to see the crown of the baby's head as it started to show.

"You're doing great, Kylie!" she gushed. "It's like you are a natural at this."

Kylie let out an exhausted laugh before bearing down again.

Each contraction pushed the head out a little farther. Brie looked across at Faelan and smiled, profoundly touched to be a part of this personal moment.

She noticed tears in his eye.

Focusing on Kylie, Faelan told her proudly, "You're doing great, baby!"

Kylie screamed with effort as she pushed even harder. Finally, the baby's head popped out.

"Just one more push to get past the shoulders, lass," Dr. Glas encouraged her.

Kylie's gaze never left Faelan as she braced herself. Her face turned a deeper shade of red as she pushed with everything she had left.

As soon as the shoulders were free, the baby slipped easily into the doctor's waiting hands.

Unlike Hope, this baby started crying immediately, filling the room with the welcomed sound.

Doctor Glas laid the infant on Kylie's chest and said with a crooked smile, "Meet your daughter, Mr. and Mrs. Wallace."

"A girl?" Kylie gasped as she stared down at the tiny baby lying on her chest.

The child instantly quieted down as soon as she was in her mother's arms.

Faelan chuckled. "Well, I didn't see that one coming...guess we'll be redecorating the nursery." Leaning in, he stroked his daughter's head. "But I'm not complaining. She's just as beautiful as her mama."

"Look how alert she is," Brie commented as the baby stared intently at Kylie.

"A little girl..." Kylie giggled softly.

After giving them several minutes to bond, Dr. Glas clamped the cord and handed Faelan a pair of surgical scissors. "It's time to cut the umbilical cord, Papa."

With a look of determination, Faelan took the scissors and cut it cleanly.

"Nicely done," Dr. Glas praised. "Many first-time fathers aren't so sure of themselves and hack at the cord, not realizing how dense it actually is."

Faelan gazed down intently at his daughter. "I wasn't about to mess it up. I'll never do anything to endanger our little girl."

Dr. Glas grinned. "Fortunately, even if you had, it wouldn't have hurt the babe. However, I appreciate your resolve."

The nurse picked up the tiny infant to weigh and assess her.

"You did exceptionally well, Mrs. Wallace," Dr. Glas complimented. "Now what are you going to name her?"

Kylie looked over at Faelan and laughed in disbelief. "We never even discussed girl names."

Faelan smirked. "Teach us to trust science."

"You've got twenty-four hours to figure it out. No pressure." Dr. Glas winked as he settled between Kylie's legs to stitch her perineum.

Once he was finished, the nurse handed Kylie back the tiny baby, now swaddled in a blanket.

"Let's give the happy family a few minutes of privacy," Dr. Glas stated.

Brie was still riding on the emotional high of witnessing the birth and stared at Kylie and Faelan, her heart bursting with happiness. Wanting to give them time alone, she excused herself. "I'll leave you two alone and tell Sir the happy news."

"Oh no, Brie. Please stay a little longer," Kylie begged. "You haven't gotten a chance to say hello yet."

Brie looked at her and then Faelan. "Are you sure?"

He smiled reassuringly. "Whatever this mama wants is fine with me."

Brie walked to the bed and leaned in to see their precious daughter. "Hello, you little cutie."

She glanced at Kylie. "It's amazing how much she looks like you."

"You think so?" Kylie smiled, obviously pleased to hear it.

"Yes," Faelan agreed. "She's the spitting image of you, my love."

"I just want to see her little fingers and toes," Kylie said wistfully.

"There's no reason you can't," Brie assured her. "They swaddle them tightly to keep the baby calm, but there's no harm in her mama taking a peek."

Kylie carefully loosened the blanket and freed her tiny hands and feet. "Oh, my goodness. Look how perfect they are."

Brie saw the flash of pride in Faelan's eyes. "Perfect."

Kylie stared up at him, shaking her head in amazement. "We did this! Can you believe it? We made this little bundle of cuteness."

He chuckled. "You did all of the work. I just enjoyed the benefits."

"I love you," she murmured, tears filling her eyes.

Reaching down, Faelan caressed Kylie's cheek. "I love you more than I can say."

Kylie smiled. "Me, too."

With Brie's help, she wrapped the baby back up.

Staring at her, Kylie laughed. "I still can't believe we have a little girl."

Brie got out her phone and instructed Faelan to get closer to Kylie so she could take a picture. "No need to say cheese. The looks on your faces say everything."

She took several pictures and then looked at them, murmuring, "Adorable." As she was putting her phone away, an alarm sounded on the monitor. She looked up and saw Kylie was suddenly as white as a ghost.

Kylie stared at Faelan and whispered, "Help…"

Kylie

After she cried for help, Kylie's body suddenly went limp and the baby rolled off her chest, getting wedged against the railing of the bed.

"Kylie!" Faelan screamed, grabbing her.

Brie picked up the wailing child and backed away, staring at Kylie in horror as alarms sounded all around them.

Dr. Glas came rushing in with a team of people and a crash cart and began barking orders.

Faelan shouted at him, "Help her, God damn it!"

The room erupted into pure chaos. Brie just stood frozen in place as memories of Tono dying in the recovery room flashed in her mind.

"You need to get out of here. You're in my way!" Dr. Glas told Faelan. The desperation Brie heard in the doctor's voice frightened her.

Faelan yelled at Dr. Glas. "You have to save her!"

"That's what I'm trying to do!"

"Kylie!" Faelan screamed in anguish, reaching out to her.

One of the nurses whipped the baby out of Brie's

hands and headed out the door. Understanding how dire the situation was, Brie grabbed Faelan and pulled him out of the room. "We have to give Dr. Glas room to work."

Once in the hallway, Brie wrapped her arms around him as they listened to the staff frantically working on Kylie.

One of the other nurses tried to direct them to the waiting room, but Faelan refused to budge. "I'm not leaving my wife!"

Knowing nothing would convince him to leave Kylie's side, Brie assured the nurse by saying, "I'll make sure we stay out of the way."

Faelan stiffened when Dr. Glas shouted to his staff, "Charge to 300. Clear!"

The sound of the defibrillator echoed through the open door. Brie whimpered when the terrifying whining of the monitor continued without any change.

Each second was agony.

"Again!" Dr. Glas commanded. "Clear!"

Faelan squeezed Brie tighter as the minutes passed, a sense of dread consuming them both.

Come back, Kylie! Please come back! Brie begged silently.

Dr. Glas worked tirelessly trying to get Kylie's heart beating again.

It came as a shock when Dr. Glas finally announced to his team, "I have tried everything I can and am ready to call the code. Anybody else have anything?"

Brie heard Faelan gasp.

The question was met with silence by the staff.

"Okay…" Dr. Glas sighed from exhaustion and defeat. "Code called at 4:52."

The nurses began the process of removing all of the

monitors. Brie saw the tears in Dr. Glas's eyes when he turned to leave and noticed the two of them standing just outside the doorway.

He joined them in the hall. "We did everything we could to save her, but she's gone. I'm…" He cleared his throat, his voice gruff with sorrow. "I'm profoundly sorry."

Faelan stared at him in silence, the shock of her death not registering.

Brie's voice quavered when she asked, "What happened?"

"She suffered a cardiac arrest."

"How is that possible?" Faelan demanded.

Dr. Glas frowned, shaking his head. "Her vitals were excellent the entire delivery. I have to assume it was a blood clot. They're known to cause ischemia during labor."

He put his hand on Faelan's shoulder, looking at him with profound sorrow. "I wish I'd been able to save her."

Faelan stared past him into the room, his voice distant. "I never got the chance to say goodbye."

Dr. Glas immediately ordered the nurses to stop what they were doing and leave the room. "Please take as much time as you need."

Faelan entered the room and slowly shut the door behind him.

Brie couldn't breathe as she turned and walked to the waiting room. She felt completely numb, but the moment she saw Sir, the tears began to fall.

"What happened?" Sir asked, rushing to her.

"Kylie's gone…" she muttered, not believing it.

"Come," Sir insisted, escorting her to a private room

set aside for grieving families.

As soon as they were alone, Brie unleashed her tears. She grabbed onto Sir, sobbing uncontrollably, completely rocked by Kylie's unexpected death.

"How did this happen?" he asked her gently.

She swallowed several times, trying to find her voice. "Dr. Glas said it was cardiac arrest." She looked up at him, her bottom lip trembling. "One moment she was smiling at her baby, and the next I hear her cry 'Help' and she was gone."

She pressed her head into his chest. "There was nothing they could do…"

"Oh, my God," Sir groaned. "What about the baby?"

"She's completely healthy."

"'She?'"

"Turns out the ultrasound was wrong. They have a little girl."

They have… The present tense no longer applied now that Kylie was gone, and Brie broke into a fresh set of tears.

"Was it a complicated delivery?" he asked gruffly. Brie could tell Sir was struggling with the shock of Kylie's death.

"No…" she whimpered. "It was an easy birth."

He squeezed her tighter. "I can only imagine what Wallace is going through right now."

Brie nodded, choking out, "He's living out the nightmare I almost experienced with you…" A sob escaped her lips. "I don't know how he is going to survive this."

Sir handed her several tissues, stating with compassion, "Wallace has friends and family who will support him."

While Brie blew her nose and wiped away her tears, Sir called Marquis on his cell to let him know what had happened.

After a short conversation, he hung up and told her, "Gray and Celestia are coming."

"Good." Brie nodded, feeling numb. "He will need their strength."

Lifting her chin, Sir looked into her eyes. "I know this is difficult for you, Brie. You've been through so much today. But, for Wallace's sake, you will need to be strong. It is not only Wallace we need to protect, but their baby."

Fresh tears welled up in her eyes. "At least he has her…"

Sir nodded, but she noticed the troubled look in his eyes.

"What are you worried about?"

"If I were in his position, I would find it difficult to care for the child. Especially in his current state—"

Sir was interrupted by a light rap on the door. He told Brie to stay where she was while he walked over to open it.

One of the nurses informed him, "Mr. Wallace would like to speak with you." He glanced over at Brie. "With both of you."

Sir held out his hand to Brie. "Are you ready?"

Brie swallowed hard but nodded. Taking a deep breath, she forced down her heartache and wiped away her remaining tears with a huge wad of tissues. Throwing them in the wastebasket, she took Sir's hand and headed out the door.

The nurse escorted them directly to Dr. Glas's private office.

Sir informed her, "We have two friends of his coming. Could you bring them here when they arrive?"

"Certainly."

When they entered the room, Brie saw Faelan standing near the window staring down at the courtyard below.

He glanced at them briefly before looking out the window again. His voice sounded hollow when he finally spoke. "I can't believe it. One moment Kylie and I are celebrating the birth of our child and the next she is gone." He lowered his head. "But she can't be gone."

"Is there anything we can do for you?" Sir asked.

Faelan shrugged, looking out the window again. With a tone of finality, he said, "There is nothing anyone can do."

Brie felt the immense pain radiating from him and struggled not to break down again. She knew from her own experience that nothing could ease the agony he was suffering right now.

"I don't want this," he stated, staring out the window.

Sir looked at him with sympathy. "It's a reality no one should have to face."

A lone tear rolled down Faelan's cheek. "The last thing she said was 'Help'." He let out a strangled cry. "I couldn't do anything but watch her die."

Brie swallowed hard, trying to keep the painful lump in her throat from choking her as images of Kylie's last seconds replayed in her mind.

"There was nothing you could do," Sir assured him.

Faelan turned on Sir, pounding his chest. "It was my job to protect her! She had a bad feeling the entire day, but I assumed she felt that way because it was her first time."

"We all did," Brie choked out.

"I didn't listen to her!" he growled, turning away from them both. "And now she's dead."

Brie felt the hairs rise on her neck. Faelan was talking as if he was responsible for her death. "This is a tragedy, Faelan. It's no one's fault."

He turned to face Brie. When he met her gaze, the depth of his pain paralyzed her. "You heard her, Brie. How many times did she tell us she was afraid?"

Brie's lip trembled when she recalled the fear in Kylie's voice. Sir put his arms around her in support.

"You did everything you could to comfort your wife," Sir told him, adding firmly, "You are not at fault."

Faelan shook his head and turned to stare out the window in silence. They remained that way until there was a knock on the door and Marquis Gray and Celestia walked into the room.

When Marquis entered and saw Faelan, he walked straight over and held out his arms in a fatherly gesture.

Faelan hesitated for a moment before accepting the embrace, muttering, "She's gone, Asher..."

Brie closed her eyes, trying desperately to keep back the flood of tears. The rawness of watching Kylie die, a young mother with so much to live for, had her heart completely shattered.

"Can I pray for you?" Marquis asked him.

When Faelan nodded, Marquis motioned all of them to join him.

Laying his hand on Faelan's shoulder, Marquis said in a powerful voice, "Lord, you said those who mourn will be comforted. We ask that you send your comfort now. Wrap Todd in your arms and hold him tight. Be with him in his sorrow, uphold him with your strength and, through the generosity of love shown by others, may he know he is not alone."

They stood as one, silently grieving Kylie's death.

The silence was broken when they heard a light rap on the door. One of the neonatal nurses peeked, in holding the baby. "I'm sorry to disturb you, but it's time to feed her. Would you like—?"

Faelan immediately answered, "No..." He choked on the words when he added, "...not yet."

She looked at him with compassion and turned to leave.

"Please, bring the child here," Marquis stated. "I would like to meet her."

The nurse hesitated until Faelan nodded his approval.

Marquis held out his hands and took the infant, gesturing to Celestia to join him. She smiled down at the child, taking her tiny hand. "Aren't you a precious thing?"

Brie remembered how intently the baby had stared at Kylie just a few hours ago. It crushed her to know this little baby would never know her mother.

It was horribly unfair.

Tears pricking her eyes, Brie fought against them, not wanting to add to Faelan's pain.

Marquis looked down at the child and smiled warmly. "Welcome to the world, little one."

The baby squirmed in his arms and began to cry.

Celestia gently asked Faelan, "Would it be okay if the nurse instructed me on how to feed her? I've never had the privilege before."

Letting out a long, anguished sigh, Faelan turned and

stared out the window. After several seconds, he gave a curt nod.

Celestia quietly followed the nurse out of the room with the fussing baby. They left a painful silence in their wake.

"What am I supposed to do?" Faelan demanded angrily. "This was supposed to be the best day of our lives." His whole body started shaking. "I can't go back to an empty home. I won't!"

"I would like you and your daughter to stay with us," Marquis answered evenly.

Faelan turned on him, narrowing his eyes. "You can't make this all better, Asher."

Marquis met his intense gaze without flinching. "No, I can't."

"I want my wife back! I want..." His voice trailed off. "...Kylie to be fucking here with me."

Brie choked on the growing lump in her throat. "I'm so sorry, Faelan."

He glanced at her. "You were there. You're the only one who understands."

She nodded, filled with overwhelming grief. "I can't believe she's gone."

"Kylie is everything to me," he stated, his gaze boring into her.

"I know," Brie whispered.

"She is the one who got me through the heartbreak after Mary. She's the one who helped me heal from the guilt of killing Trevor." Faelan unconsciously brushed the eye patch on his left eye, "She made me whole again after Russia. I became a better man because of her." He stared back out the window. "But none of it matters now."

Brie felt a prickling sensation when she heard his last words.

"It does matter," Sir insisted. "You have a child to care for."

Faelan turned on him, his eyes flashing in a warning. "Don't even go there…"

Instead of backing down, Sir moved closer. "You don't have the luxury of giving up, Wallace. You have a daughter who needs you."

Faelan howled in rage, slamming Sir's chest hard with both fists. The impact pushed him backward.

Sir steadied himself and looked Faelan in the eye. "Do that again."

"Are you seriously trying to provoke me at a time like this? What the fuck is wrong with you!"

"Now is not the time," Marquis warned Sir.

Sir raised his hand to Marquis. "Stay out of this, Gray."

Brie stared at the two men, trembling in fear.

"Hit me," Sir commanded.

Faelan sneered at him. "No."

As soon as the word left his mouth, Sir punched him.

"This is enough!" Marquis stated, moving in to intervene.

Faelan held nothing back when he started wailing on Sir. Brie stood frozen in place as she watched Sir take Faelan's pent-up fury without attempting to defend himself.

Eventually, Faelan stopped, panting heavily as he stared Sir down.

Sir slowly wiped the blood from his lip. "Your wife is dead. It's okay to cry."

Faelan backed away from him as if he'd been hit. Shaking his head, he turned and retreated to a corner. After several moments, his shoulders began to shake as a heart-wrenching sob escaped his lips.

Sir walked to him, wrapping an arm around Faelan in support as he roared out in pain, releasing the anger and shock of Kylie's death.

Hearing his raw anguish tore at Brie's heart—the sound of it was something she would never forget.

Marquis joined Brie. He hugged her tightly, imparting his strength, as they stood back and listened to Faelan's desperate cries of grief.

Dr. Glas appeared, opening his office door with a concerned look on his face. As soon as he saw Faelan was being comforted, he quietly withdrew. However, Brie did not miss the look of torment in the doctor's eyes when he'd glanced at her before closing it.

It was obvious he was tormented by Kylie's death as well.

So many lives shattered on a day that should have been a celebration.

Hours later, Sir was able to convince Faelan to leave the hospital. He refused to see the baby when the nurse asked.

"I need time to adjust to this," he explained.

After she left the room, he frowned. "Right now, I would switch out the baby for Kylie in a heartbeat." He muttered, "The child doesn't deserve that..."

Before he was allowed to leave, Faelan was handed a

form and instructed, "You'll need to fill out the birth certificate and get it to us when you come to pick her up tomorrow."

Faelan stared blankly at the piece of paper, then said in a strangled voice, "We never came up with a name for her."

Marquis clapped him on the shoulder, taking the paper from him. "There is time for everything. Right now, you need to rest."

Faelan shook his head, choking out the words. "Oh, God… I have to call Kylie's parents."

"I'll call them," Sir replied.

Faelan nodded, saying nothing as he unlocked his phone and handed it over.

After Sir had added the number to his and handed it back, Celestia slipped her arm around Faelan. "Let's get you out of here."

Before he left, Faelan turned to Sir. "How did you know to do that?"

"Do what?"

"Force me to hit you."

Sir answered with a grave smile. "Durov did something similar to me in college. There are times when the only way to release pain is to inflict it."

Faelan nodded, then looked down at the floor for a moment. He met Sir's gaze again and said, "I may need another session with you."

Sir rubbed his jaw. "Anytime."

After they left, Brie and Sir walked to the hospital nursery and gazed at the tiny baby swaddled in a pink blanket with the name *Wallace, Baby Girl* attached to the crib over her head.

"I'm so sad for her," Brie said, tears rolling down her

cheeks.

Sir put his arm around her, kissing the top of her head. "We can't change what happened today, but we can commit to giving this child and Wallace the support they need."

Brie shuddered. She turned into his embrace and held him tight. "I keep thinking that this was almost my fate—raising Hope without you."

Sir placed his hand firmly on her stomach. "I am not going anywhere, babygirl."

Tribute

As they drove home from the hospital, Brie stared out of the car window. Although she tried, she couldn't stop replaying Kylie's last few moments in her head. There had been nothing to indicate anything was wrong. Even Dr. Glas hadn't been worried.

With the miracle of modern medicine, Brie never considered she could die during childbirth, and a chill of fear set in as she looked down at her stomach.

By the time they reached Rytsar's home, Brie was in desperate need to hold Hope. She raced out of the car and started pounding on the door.

Rytsar was the one who answered it. The look of sympathy in his eyes alerted Brie to the fact that Sir had already texted him about what had happened.

"Where's Hope?" she whimpered before he could even speak.

Rytsar pointed to the living room. Hope was on the floor, petting Little Sparrow. The pup's eyes were half-closed, looking as if she was in dog heaven.

Brie ran to Hope, tears running down her face. She picked up her little girl and squeezed her against her chest. Never in her life, other than the day she was born, had Brie been so grateful to hold her little girl.

"I am sorry, *radost moya*," Rytsar said gently, coming up behind her.

Brie nodded, but the emotions bubbled up once more making it impossible to speak.

She lowered her head, rocking Hope in her arms to keep from falling apart.

"It has been a harrowing day," Sir said, laying his hand on her shoulder in comfort.

Rytsar glanced at his swollen jaw. "It looks like it was for you as well, *moy droog*."

Sir gestured to his face. "What, this? This is nothing."

Rytsar frowned in concern. "Would vodka help?"

Brie felt the dam of her emotions starting to break and shook her head vigorously. Needing solitude, she walked to Rytsar's bedroom with Hope and lay down on his bed.

Hope stared at her questioningly as silent tears rolled down her face onto the pillow. When she reached out and touched Brie's wet cheek, the innocent contact caused a painful sob to escape Brie's lips, shattering her last vestige of control.

Brie pulled Hope closer as the immense sorrow she felt for Kylie caused a torrent of tears to unleash. The pain that followed consumed her until she felt the bed sink on both sides.

In an act of quiet solidarity, Rytsar and Sir joined her on the bed, fully clothed, and wrapped their protective arms around her as she hugged Hope tight.

The entire BDSM community reached out to Faelan after hearing about the tragic news, but he refused all contact with the outside world.

Even Brie and Sir were advised by Marquis not to visit when they spoke to him on the phone, but he assured them, "He is working through this difficult transition."

When Brie asked how the baby was, Marquis was silent.

"Is the child okay?" Sir asked with concern.

Marquis took a moment before answering. "The baby is healthy and is being well cared for."

Brie glanced at Sir, sensing Marquis Gray was keeping something from them.

Sir repeated their commitment to help. "What can we do?"

"Nothing at the moment, Sir Davis. But if you feel inclined, pray for him."

Brie felt uneasy when they hung up. "What is Marquis not telling us?"

Sir looked equally troubled. "For now, we must trust Gray to guide Wallace through this. Once we see him in person at the funeral, we will be able to better judge if Faelan needs our intervention."

In the days leading up to the funeral, Brie was plagued by formless nightmares. She could never remember her dreams, but a feeling of darkness and despair permeated her soul the moment she woke, completely terrifying her. She was certain that, on some subconscious level, she was picking up on Faelan's state of mind while she slept.

The morning of the service, Brie attempted to put on her makeup with trembling hands. The idea she was attending Kylie's funeral seemed unreal—being so young, and a new mother.

Kylie deserved to be there to love and care for her child. Brie could not accept that life could be that cruel.

As Sir straightened his tie beside her, he said, "I know today will be extremely difficult, but Wallace will depend on your strength."

She turned to Sir with sad eyes and nodded.

He held out his arms to her. "I know you are fighting many emotions right now, babygirl. You're not only dealing with the loss of your friend, but I'm certain it reconnects you with the heavy emotions my own brush with death caused you. Added to that is the overwhelming concern you have for Wallace's wellbeing."

Her bottom lip quivered, astonished that he understood. "How did you know?"

Sir caressed her cheek. "Every emotion plays out on your beautiful face."

Brie closed her eyes, uncertain if she would be strong enough for the day and what lay ahead. She immediately squashed the thought.

Of course, she could do this. It paled in comparison to what Faelan had to face today. Brie stared into the mirror while she finished getting ready. Fate gave a person opportunities in their life to make a difference. No one would blame Brie for being an emotional wreck at the funeral, but that would be of no help to Faelan.

Looking up at Sir, she felt a surge of conviction. Faelan needed her, and she would not fail him.

Sir leaned down to kiss her lightly on the lips, whispering, "Heart of a warrior."

With newfound determination, Brie kissed Sir on the cheek before heading out of the bedroom.

The Reynolds had asked to watch Hope. They wanted to support Faelan by keeping the children at home.

Judy grabbed Brie's hands when she saw her. "I want you to think of Hope playing with Jonathan when things get too hard today. I hope, in some way, it will help."

Brie nodded, overcome with gratitude. "It will. Thank you."

Jack shook his head in sorrow. "Such a tragedy. Kylie was a positive light in the world. I hate to think what a blow this is to Todd."

"One can only imagine," Sir answered solemnly.

Judy handed Sir a card. "Would you mind making sure he gets this? We want him to know we are happy to babysit his little girl anytime he needs it." She looked at her husband. "It's one of the perks of being retired, and we hope it will give him peace of mind to know his daughter will be well cared for."

"I will be certain to give it to him, Auntie." Sir slipped the card into the pocket of his suit.

Jack put his hand on Sir's back. "You've been through hell yourself, so I'm confident you can help him through this, Thane."

"I hate that he must face this." Sir sighed sadly. "I owe the man in more ways than I can count and I am prepared to do whatever is necessary to help."

"Todd is fortunate to have good people supporting him," Jack replied, patting his back one last time before picking up Hope's car seat and heading to the door.

Sir followed them to the door and smiled at Hope before leaning down to kiss her on the head. "Goodbye, sweet angel."

On the drive to the funeral, Brie reflected on how selfless Faelan had been when he agreed to act as her protector after Rytsar was abducted. He even volunteered to travel to Russia in an attempt to save Rytsar, knowing he might not come back—and he did not come back the same man.

Yet, Faelan faced the consequences of his decisions without complaint. Today, he would need her to be just as selfless. Steeling herself for the day, Brie practiced her breathing.

"Are you okay, babygirl?"

She turned her head to meet his gaze. "I will be."

He nodded in encouragement.

So many people attended Kylie's funeral, it was standing room only. Although Brie and Sir arrived early, they sat in the far back. Brie could barely see Faelan up at the front.

He sat, hunched over, his face buried in his hands. Marquis sat beside him, his hand on Faelan's back. On the opposite side of Marquis, Celestia sat rocking the tiny infant.

Glancing around the room, Brie saw many faces she recognized, including Dr. Glas, who was standing on the other side of the room. Brie was pleased to see the doctor had come in support. Although she thought it unusual, she found it touching and was comforted by his presence.

The entire room was silent except for the occasional cough and quiet sniffles. The mood of the gathering was intensely somber as everyone stared at the closed coffin and the beautiful portrait of Kylie beside it. She was beaming at everyone in attendance with her winning smile.

Brie understood why Faelan couldn't bear to look at it.

Even though it was held in a church, it was not a heavily religious ceremony. Instead, it was about celebrating Kylie's life and the people she had touched. Brie heard that her parents had spent days creating the video of Kylie, which they played during the service.

For the first time, Brie saw pictures of Kylie as a baby. It struck Brie how closely her daughter resembled her, with those big expressive eyes and that cute button nose.

Gut-wrenching sobs came from up front as both families mourned for her loss, but Faelan remained silent, hunched over with his head lowered.

When the pastor invited people to speak, Kylie's brother was the first to come forward. He shared memories of their childhood and the fact that Kylie graduated top of her class. What he remembered most, however, was the excitement in Kylie's voice when she confessed she'd found the man she was going to marry when she was still in high school. That had stayed with him because she did end up marrying him before she died.

"I've never seen a woman more in love," her brother confessed, glancing at Faelan.

All eyes turned to him, but Faelan kept his face buried in his hands, oblivious to everyone around him.

Unfazed, Kylie's bother continued but, partway through his eulogy, the baby started to fuss. When Celestia's efforts failed and she couldn't quiet her, both grandmothers attempted to comfort the child to no avail.

Faelan made no move to quiet the child.

Brie felt sad for the baby but understood. All she had to do was put herself in Faelan's place to realize he was in too much pain to help anyone—even his little girl.

Once Celestia had her quiet again, the service continued without interruption. Normally, immediately following the funeral, the grieving family stood outside to greet those in attendance and allow them to express their condolences.

However, at the end of this service, Marquis stood up and addressed everyone in attendance.

"Honoring the wishes of the family, we ask that you make your way to your cars. We will follow the limousine to the cemetery where there will be a short graveside service."

Marquis then placed his hand on Faelan's shoulder.

Faelan glanced up at Marquis with a look of relief. He stood up and hurried out of the back of the church without saying a word to anyone.

"This does not bode well," Sir murmured under his breath as they filed out of the church.

"I agree, Sir," Brie whimpered.

Sir rested his hand on Brie's shoulder as they waited for Marquis and Celestia to emerge from the church.

Rytsar joined them. "The boy is not well."

Sir frowned. "It's far worse than I thought."

"What are we going to do, *moy droog*?"

"We need to speak to Wallace alone."

"Agreed."

When Marquis and Celestia finally appeared, the three walked over to join them. Celestia was dabbing her eyes as they approached, while Marquis Gray held the tiny baby.

"It was a beautiful service, but my heart is utterly

broken," Celestia confessed, unable to stop her tears.

Brie immediately hugged her, squeezing her tight.

"We are concerned about Wallace," Sir told Marquis.

"As you should be, he's been inconsolable since her death." Marquis glanced at his wife. "Celestia hasn't been able to get him to eat anything."

Brie looked at Marquis in alarm.

Celestia stared at the tiny baby in Marquis Gray's arms. "He won't even look at the child."

"It sounds like he's given up," Rytsar stated.

"I'm afraid that is the case," Marquis said solemnly. "He is seeing a therapist under my advisement, but…it doesn't seem to be enough."

Celestia looked at Sir with concern. "I'm afraid he may end up in the hospital if things don't change soon."

"We won't let that happen," Rytsar assured her.

Turning to Brie, Marquis said, "Faelan has mentioned you several times. It seems he feels connected to you since you were both there when she passed."

Tears welled up in Brie's eyes as she remembered that moment. She had to swallow twice before she could speak. Clearing her throat, she asked him, "What can I do, Marquis Gray?"

He took a few moments to consider. "I get the impression you are the only one he might open up to."

Marquis Gray turned to Sir. "However, I am uncertain how that would play out. The three of you have a complicated history."

"Are you talking about the fact that he loved Brie once?"

Marquis nodded.

Glancing at Brie, Sir stated, "I am confident my wife can navigate those waters. If the interaction became unhealthy, she would simply disengage."

To Marquis, he said, "Brie and I are both committed to helping Wallace in whatever capacity needed."

"Then I suggest you come to the house tonight after he's had a chance to recover from the strain of this gathering." Marquis looked at both of them, adding, "I am grateful to you."

When the limousine pulled up to the front of the church, Marquis handed the baby to Celestia and shook Sir and Rytsar's hands, nodding to Brie respectfully.

As Sir escorted Brie to their car, she noticed Mary quietly talking with Lea and Hunter. It made sense that Mary was here to support Faelan, but Brie wondered what she was feeling.

When Mary glanced her way, Brie smiled sadly at her. Mary nodded in response and bumped Lea. When Lea looked up and saw Brie, she put her hand over her heart and mouthed the words, *we love you.*

Brie appreciated having her friends' support. It gave her the boost she needed as she got into the car and they joined the long procession of vehicles with their lights on. Because it was such a large turnout, the cars stretched out for almost half a mile.

It was a moving tribute to Kylie, but so horribly tragic.

Confessions

It took considerable time for everyone to gather at the burial site because so many had come. Faelan stayed in the limousine while they waited for people who'd parked far away to walk to the grave.

Sir used the time to go up to Faelan's parents to offer their condolences. The moment Faelan's mother saw him, she immediately threw her arms around him. "Mr. Davis, it is always a blessing to see you, even at a terrible time like this."

The couple looked even more beaten and frail than they had when Brie had met them at the hospital several years ago before Faelan's kidney surgery.

Mr. Wallace gave Sir and Brie a firm handshake. "You two gave us our son back, we will forever be grateful." Glancing at the darkened windows of the limousine, he muttered, "I only hope you can help him now."

"We'll do everything in our power," Sir assured him.

"He seems unreachable this time," Mrs. Wallace whimpered, wiping tears from her eyes.

"Losing Kylie is more…" Brie started choking up.

"…than he can bear."

Mrs. Wallace grabbed Brie's hand. "I heard that you were there. It must have been terrible."

Brie held the tears back, determined to be strong for all of them. "I'm glad he wasn't alone."

"Poor Kylie," Faelan's father said, swiping hastily at his eyes.

"It's a tragedy on all accounts," Sir stated, putting his arm around Brie. She was grateful for the physical support.

"The baby is healthy," Mr. Wallace said gruffly. "We take comfort in that."

"She is a beautiful little girl," Brie agreed.

"I wish Todd would hold her…" Mrs. Wallace sniffed.

Brie gave Sir a worried look. She hadn't realized Faelan wasn't interacting with his child at all.

Mr. Wallace walked them to Kylie's parents and introduced them.

Brie could barely look her mother in the eyes, aware of the pain she was suffering. Feeling the need to comfort her, Brie wrapped her arms around the grieving woman. "I'm so sorry."

The woman grew stiff in Brie's arms and only nodded.

Kylie's father asked Brie in a choked voice. "How was she…at the end?"

Brie had prepared herself for the question and answered in the gentlest way she could. "She was happy. I will never forget the joy on her face when she held her daughter or the way your granddaughter looked at her with such love."

"She didn't die in pain?" Kylie's mother whimpered.

Brie kept her smile even though she knew her answer would be hard for the parents to hear. "Kylie did cry out for help. It was as if she could sense something was wrong just before she passed out, but she didn't suffer."

Her parents nodded, tears rolling down their cheeks.

"Kylie was well-loved by many, as you can see," Sir stated in a warm voice. "I hope that brings you some comfort."

Her father glanced around at the number of people still walking up to the gravesite. "People here have been exceedingly kind to us. So yes, Mr. Davis, it does ease our pain to know she was surrounded by good people."

Once everyone had gathered, Marquis went back to the limousine to get Faelan.

He stepped out of the vehicle, a look of anguish on his face, and slowly approached the grave. His eyes were locked on it as if he didn't see anyone or anything else.

Taking his place between both sets of parents, Faelan stood with his hands behind his back and his head bowed. He remained that way for the entire graveside service. He didn't move or make a sound, although everyone around him sobbed. But Brie could feel his torment and noticed the tears that silently fell to the ground.

When the time came to lower the coffin into the ground, Faelan suddenly stiffened and closed his eyes. He remained where he was while everyone else threw handfuls of dirt onto the coffin in honor of her.

Brie could feel the building tension he was throwing off.

Suddenly, Faelan dropped to his knees and cried out, "Don't leave me here alone!"

The anguish in his voice sent chills through Brie.

Everyone froze, caught in the intensity of his pain.

Marquis and Faelan's father quietly helped him to his feet. Together, they attempted to lead him back to the limousine, but he broke from their grip, howling angrily as he stormed away in the opposite direction. People hastily made a path for him through the crowd.

Sir touched Brie's shoulder. "Go to him."

Brie glanced up at Sir, tears in her eyes, and nodded. Hurrying after Faelan, she had to force her way through the stunned crowd.

When she finally caught up to him, he growled ominously, "Leave me alone, Brie."

"Okay," she answered, but she continued walking three steps behind him.

Finally, he turned on her. "I told you to leave me the fuck alone!"

Brie met his gaze. "I am."

"No, you're not! You're still following me."

He marched away from her at a faster pace.

She glanced at the crowd and saw they were all watching in concern. She waited several seconds to give him more space before following him again.

"I can still hear you," he snarled without looking back.

Brie understood what he wanted but felt compelled to continue.

When they were far from the grave, he stopped and turned to face her. The grief on his face had transformed into rage. "I don't want you here!"

She stood quietly, not daring to move, afraid if she did she might evoke his rage to explode.

"I don't want this. I don't want any of it!" he yelled.

"I know…" she whispered desperately.

The raw pain in his ocean blue eye ripped at her heart.

"I would trade places with her without hesitation," he declared angrily.

Brie nodded, holding back her tears although her heart was breaking for him.

Faelan gestured toward the direction of the gravesite. "I didn't want a funeral, but Kylie deserved to be honored. It's the only reason I agreed to come." His voice faltered. "But now, I regret it…"

"Why?" she whispered, desperate to understand.

His blue eye pierced her soul. "It makes it final. I'm alone now."

Goosebumps rose on her skin. "You have a beautiful daughter."

"Just being near her cuts me like a knife," he snarled.

"But she's a part of Kylie."

He glared at Brie. "Exactly. She reminds me of everything I've lost."

Faelan turned from Brie, a low moan escaping his lips. "I'm haunted by the fear in her voice when she cried out for help."

Brie closed her eyes, ice running through her veins. She couldn't forget Kylie's plaintive cry. Swallowing hard, she forced herself to speak. "I remember how she was bursting with love for your daughter. That's what I hold onto now."

Faelan shook his head.

He tensed when Brie placed her hand on his back. "I have a secret I have carried with me since Hope's birth."

He turned around, looking at her questioningly.

"You know I love Thane as much as you love Kylie."

He furrowed his brow in pain but nodded.

"Like you, I can't imagine a future without him. But when Hope's heart-rate started to drop dangerously low while giving birth, I silently begged for my life to be taken so hers would be spared. I know that Kylie felt the same way about your little girl."

He shook his head violently, but Brie said firmly, "Faelan, I would have gladly given up my life with Sir, because Hope is more important than either of us."

"No!"

Brie smiled at him compassionately. "Your little girl was created out of love and is a part of you both."

"I have a secret of my own, Brie."

She held her breath, troubled by his somber tone.

Letting out a ragged sigh, he confessed, "I wish the baby had never been born."

They stood together in silence as the truth filled the space between them.

Although his words sounded heartless, Brie knew it was his love for Kylie that spurred them.

Faelan shook his head angrily. "She *knew* something terrible was going to happen and I ignored her."

"No! Dr. Glas said her vitals were good. How many times did he check in on her? And she always said she was fine but nervous. Kylie didn't know any more than we did."

"She was terrified, Brie. *That's* why she asked you to come." He groaned. "And now, we know why…"

Brie understood he was condemning himself for what happened. She suspected he was replaying every aspect of the day, questioning every decision he made, wondering what he could have done to prevent her from dying.

She knew from experience that what-ifs served no

purpose.

"Faelan, I remember something Captain told me after the plane crash. It seemed coldhearted when he said it back then, but it has carried me through some difficult moments since."

"What?" Faelan asked, his voice gruff with emotion.

"It is never wise to concern ourselves with what-ifs."

He growled, not appreciating Captain's simple but profound advice.

Brie continued, "Your daughter is depending on you, Faelan. You have to concentrate on recovering from this unexpected loss. She needs her father to be well."

He frowned, shaking his head as he stared at the ground. "I am a man of extremes, Brie. When I love, I'm all in." He glanced up at her. "I was that way with you and Mary. But Kylie was different because she loved me back with the same intensity I loved her."

Tears pricked Brie's eyes as she nodded.

"Kylie was everything to me, my best parts. I'm nothing without her."

Brie reached out to him. "That's not true."

He looked her dead in the eye. "You want the real truth?"

She nodded, holding her breath.

"Now that she's gone, my only thought—my only desire—is to join her."

Goosebumps rose on Brie's skin at the finality of those words. "Kylie would never want that!"

Faelan snarled. "You can't speak for her."

"I can speak as a mother. I know to the depths of my soul that Kylie would never want you to abandon your baby."

"I wasn't supposed to do this on my own!"

"I know," Brie said with compassion. "None of this was supposed to happen…but you can't give up on the one thing Kylie loved even more than you."

Fire flashed in Faelan's eyes, and he said in a cold voice, "Go away."

"Faelan, I—"

"Not another word, Brie," he warned. "Leave me the fuck alone and tell Asher to do the same."

When she didn't move, he pointed his finger. "Go now!"

Brie knew she'd hit a nerve, but she desperately hoped he would consider what she'd said. Turning away she headed back to the gravesite, her heart heavier than before.

Instead of going to Marquis Gray's house that night, Brie returned home feeling bereft.

She sat on the couch hugging her pillow for hours, completely unaware of her surroundings—lost in her sadness.

Sir finally broke through the haze, holding his hand out to her. "Come. Let your men love you."

Brie looked up to see Rytsar standing beside him.

Taking Sir's hand, Brie was pulled into his arms and the two men walked her to the bedroom.

They undressed her with gentle hands. Once naked, Sir picked her up and carried her to the bed. Both Sir and Rytsar quietly shed their clothes and joined her.

Brie felt dangerously empty—as if she were a black hole of sorrow that could consume them if they got too close.

But neither man hesitated, requiring nothing of her as they caressed her body and left trails of kisses over her skin. They were so tender in their lovemaking that it brought tears to her eyes.

"Let it out, *radost moya*," Rytsar murmured, kissing her on the lips.

Brie resisted, unwilling to submit herself to the pain, but Rytsar would not let it consume her. He slowly pressed his cock into her, filling the void in her soul.

His strokes were slow and measured—his touch tender and sweet—but she looked up at him, too numb to respond.

Never breaking eye contact with her, Rytsar rolled with Brie so they were lying on their side. Sir spooned against her, pressing his lubricated shaft into her tight resistance as he whispered. "I love you."

Brie closed her eyes, the tears squeezing through her eyelids despite her best efforts to keep them back.

The men were persistent in their love, drawing her in with their need to connect with her. There finally came a point when she could no longer resist them, and everything she'd held back came bubbling out.

"*Da*," Rytsar growled in encouragement when the tears began to fall freely.

Soon, Brie began sobbing as she gave in to their lovemaking, needing the emotional connection that taking both men at the same time created.

It sustained her as she gave in to the uncertainty and pain caused by Kylie's death. They rode out her sorrow with her, unified as one so she could bear the devastating weight of it.

The torment of her grief was matched by the

strength of their love. In that way, she withstood the tidal wave that engulfed her.

Afterward, she lay in their arms, their spent cocks still buried deep inside her. She was emotionally exhausted, but her heart was less heavy. She turned her head and gazed up at the ceiling in silence, indebted to them both for their intervention.

Brie eventually broke the silence, needing to voice her thoughts to them. "Faelan is facing my greatest fear…" She turned to look at Sir, her brows furrowed in pain. "I will never forget how terrified I was when I thought I was losing you."

Sir stared at her, his eyes full of compassion. "But you stayed strong."

Feeling profound guilt, she confessed, "I was no different than Faelan, Sir. I ignored everything, including our child…"

"It's a natural response when faced with loss," he replied. "Which is why we support Wallace now."

Rytsar spoke up. "*Radost moya*, I promise he will get through this. I am well acquainted with his hell."

She turned her head, looking at him sadly. She knew he was talking about Tatianna.

"I live with tragic loss every day. It never leaves the heart."

"I'm so sorry, Rytsar." The immensity of his loss hit her like it never had before and she started to cry again.

"Do not weep, *radost moya*. I know Tatianna waits for me. One day, I will see her again and we will be reunited."

He gently wiped away her tears. "Kylie died at the happiest point in her life. Not many are as fortunate." Rytsar frowned slightly. "However, I know Tatianna is at peace and waits patiently for me. It is the same for the Wolf Pup."

Taking Brie's hand, he placed it over his heart. "There are two kinds of people in the world. Those who live their life to the fullest because they realize they can die at any moment, and those who live their life in fear, trying to protect it. What those who live in fear fail to realize is that they are already dead."

Her bottom lip trembled.

"Surviving Tatianna's loss freed me from the fear of death because it will be welcomed when it comes."

She whimpered at the thought.

Rytsar grazed her bottom lip, smiling. "I'm in no hurry to die."

He glanced at Sir. "I made that vow a long time ago."

"Yes, you did," Sir affirmed.

Looking back at Brie, Rytsar continued, "Live your life fearlessly, *radost moya.*"

She nodded.

"Do not concern yourself with the Wolf Pup." He smiled confidently. "I will guide him to the other side of hell, whatever it takes."

Sir caressed her cheek tenderly. "I promise you, babygirl. Wallace has a band of people who will not let him down."

Remembering the lengths her friends went to supporting her after Sir's plane crash, Brie knew he was right and a feeling of profound relief washed over her.

"Now sleep and let your heart heal," Sir commanded gently.

Kindness

B rie got up to take her morning walk, wanting to speed the healing process by moving about her days as she had always done. She hoped it would bring her a sense of peace.

Although the beauty of nature surrounded her, Brie's heart still felt heavy. When she saw the old woman, she lowered her head and kept walking.

It went on like that for days, and she was sorely tempted to quit her walks and sleep in instead. But she persevered each morning, trotting along with her head down, hoodie pulled over her head.

"Hey!"

Brie barely registered that someone had spoken and kept walking.

"Hey, girl!" the person called out louder.

She stopped and turned to see the old woman. "Look. I got something for you."

Brie noticed she was clutching something. "What?"

The woman thrust out her hand. "Just take it."

As Brie walked over to her, the little dog whined but wagged its tail enthusiastically. The old woman clasped her hand and pressed her gift into it.

Brie looked down to see a used pair of socks with daisies on them. It was the first pair she had given to her.

"No matter how bad it gets you can always look at your feet."

Brie looked up at her questioningly.

The old woman pointed to her own feet. She was wearing the latest socks Brie had given her, a vibrant blue pair with cupcakes on them.

"Come, Chester," she barked, grabbing her bag of plastic bottles.

Chester looked up at Brie, wagged his tail, and yipped twice before joining the old woman.

Brie stared down at the socks in shock, certain the old woman had no idea that she was the one who had given her the socks in the first place.

This was a random act of kindness…

Tears filled her eyes as she continued to walk, deeply touched by the woman's generosity.

When she returned home, she showed the socks to Sir.

He chuckled. "So, you've finally been caught?"

Brie shook her head, looking at the used socks. "I think she wanted me to have one of her most prized possession, Sir." She looked up at him in wonder. "Just because she wanted to make me smile."

Sir took the socks from her, studying them thoughtfully. "You managed to soften a cold heart once again." He gazed into her eyes, adding, "Well done, babygirl."

Brie stood on tiptoes to kiss him. "Thank you for helping me understand what she needed."

Sir handed the socks back to her. "So, what are you going to do with them?"

"I plan to wear them tomorrow on my walk, then I'm putting them in a place of honor for safekeeping." Looking down at the tattered socks, Brie was overcome with gratefulness, treasuring the old woman's gift.

The kindness of a stranger truly had untold power.

Lea and Mary insisted on dragging Brie out for some much-needed girl time.

"Sorry, but I'm not in the mood," she apologized when they showed up at her door.

"Which is why you have no choice," Lea stated, taking her hand and escorting her outside.

Brie looked back to see Sir standing in the doorway with Hope in his arms, and realized she'd been set up.

Once the three of them were in Mary's car, Brie asked them, "Now that I've been kidnapped, where are you taking me?"

"Our old bar near the Submissive Training Center, where else?" Mary answered.

"Did you forget Brie is pregnant?" Lea chided.

Mary huffed, looking in the rearview mirror at Brie. "You are pretty useless as a friend when you're pregnant."

Brie laughed. "Excuse me for being such a burden."

"You're no such thing. Mary's just a twat."

"I may be a twat, but at least I'm funny."

It was Lea's turn to huff. "You wish."

Brie enjoyed listening to their familiar banter. There was a normalcy to it that helped lighten her spirits.

"Since we're not allowed to hang out at the bar,

where would you like to go, Stinks?"

Brie thought about it for a moment before she suddenly realized what she needed. "It's a bit far."

"Don't care."

Brie got teary, touched by what an incredible friend she was, and choked out, "Thanks, Mary."

She immediately chastised Brie. "Don't get all emotional on my account. Now give me the directions, woman."

Brie smirked, wiping her eyes.

Lea took her hand and squeezed it.

They rode in silence, her friends uncertain how to bring up the topic of Kylie's death and Brie unwilling to break the comfortable cocoon their presence provided.

When they finally reached the destination, Brie told Mary to pull over.

"You sure this is the place?"

"Yep."

Brie got out of the car and stood at the edge of the steep embankment overlooking the huge city of LA. There was only one other person she had brought up here after Sir introduced her to the place.

It had become a sacred spot for Brie.

Sir had first driven her here after an unexpected run-in with his mother. Brie glanced at the tree where he had released his anger with his fists. That night had been both terrible and hauntingly beautiful at the same time.

Brie smiled back at her girlfriends. "I brought my mother here once. Just after we found my wedding dress."

"Oh, wow, Brie. This is a killer view of Los Angeles!" Lea stepped up beside her.

Mary sauntered up behind them. "Eh, it ain't bad."

Lea gave her a hip bump. "Mary Quite Contrary."

Brie looked over the city in silence, taking strength from the life it represented.

"How are you doing, Brie?" Lea finally asked.

Still staring at the city, Brie asked, "Have you ever watched a person die?"

"No..." Lea whispered.

"It haunts me every day."

Brie pulled out her phone and showed them the photo she took at the hospital. Faelan had his arm around Kylie, both of them glowing as they looked down at their baby. "I took this just before she died."

Lea whimpered.

Ever the blunt one, Mary asked, "What was it like?"

"Her death was quick and so terribly final..." Brie glanced at the photo again. "How can a person so young and full of life be gone just like that? I still can't believe she's dead even though I was there."

Lea cried, "Poor Faelan."

"He's definitely been given a shitty hand in life," Mary muttered.

Lea looked stricken when she told them, "I heard he hasn't even held the baby."

"Faelan is really struggling," Brie confessed.

"Sometimes you reach a breaking point," Mary stated, her tone so matter-of-fact it frightened Brie.

Brie turned to her in concern, "You're not at that point, are you?"

She scoffed. "Don't worry about me, Stinks. I'm like the cat that came back the very next day. This pussy ain't going anywhere."

"I can't tell you how grateful I am for your strength, Mary."

She rolled her eyes. "Stop with all the mushy crap. You know I hate that shit."

Brie smiled.

"I'm seriously worried about Faelan, Brie," Lea said. "Is there anything we can do?"

Brie sighed, feeling equally concerned. "Keep him in your thoughts, you guys. He's shunning all contact because he's in a dark place right now."

"I feel sorry for his parents," Mary told them. "They looked completely shattered at the funeral. They're so desperate, they even asked me to reach out to their son."

"Don't they know you broke up with him?" Lea asked.

"Yeah, which just shows how desperate they are."

Brie frowned. "They have every right to worry. Even Marquis Gray is concerned."

A sense of melancholy settled over the three as they stood together, staring out at the bustling city below.

"There's only one thing to be done," Mary stated, her voice resolute.

Brie turned to her. "What?"

"It's time for big boobs to kill us with a joke."

"Is that supposed to be funny?" Lea grumbled, clearly offended.

"No. I'm being completely serious."

Brie smiled at Lea. "I could use one right now."

"Okay…"

Lea started pacing back and forth. "Give me a second you guys. I'm not prepared for this."

Mary smirked at Brie. "Who knew Lea would ever be at a loss for words?"

"I actually know a lot of jokes in sign language," Lea informed her.

"Really?" Brie asked.

"Yeah, but nobody has ever heard them," she answered as she continued to pace.

It took Brie a few moments to catch on. She glanced at Mary and saw her dragging her hands down her face in feigned agony.

Brie burst out laughing. "That joke was professionally executed, Lea. It was so subtle I nearly missed it, which makes it even funnier. Well done, girlfriend."

Lea beamed at her. "I've got a great one for you, Stinky Cheese. What do you call a threesome where one Dom praises you and the other humiliates you?"

"A good time?" Mary answered.

Lea snickered. "Of course, you'd say that."

Brie thought about it for a minute and shrugged. "You got me."

"Good Top, Bad Top."

Giggling, Brie walked over to hug Lea. "You can always make me smile."

"I aim to please."

"Well, now that I am done sacrificing myself for the greater good, I'm calling uncle," Mary told them.

Lea snorted. "I was done anyway."

"Thank God."

"Oh, you guys, I almost forgot. Hunter bought me a new blindfold but there's a problem." Lea pouted.

"What's wrong?" Brie asked, curious about what it could be.

She shrugged. "I can't see myself wearing it."

Before Brie could react, Mary let out a tortured groan. "What the hell, Lea! I called uncle."

"Gotcha!" Lea giggled, looking quite pleased with herself.

In the middle of laughing, Brie suddenly stopped short when a vision of Kylie's coffin came to her mind.

"It's okay to laugh, Stinks," Mary told her.

"I know." She let out a strangled sigh. "It's just that…"

Lea put her arms around Brie. "No need to explain yourself, girlfriend. We understand."

"I've been thinking about what you said." Mary gazed down at the LA landscape below. "If we can't help Todd right now, then we need to be there for the kid. No child should ever feel unloved."

Brie looked at Mary with compassion. Despite her brash demeanor, Mary was a wealth of depth and kindness.

"I couldn't agree more."

The next day, Rytsar came bursting into their house. "I need you both to come with me."

Sir looked up from his office desk. "Where?"

"Wallace refuses to see me, and Gray won't let me come uninvited without you."

"Unless you have a plan, I don't see the point." Sir went back to his work.

"But I do, *moy droog*! You know the special bond the Wolf Pup has with *Vorobyshek*. I am willing to give her up for the time being so she can aid him in his healing."

Brie perked up when she heard Rytsar mention his dog, Little Sparrow. "That's a great idea. He's always had a soft spot for her, and animals can reach people in ways humans can't."

"It certainly has a chance of working," Sir agreed. "Give me a couple of minutes to finish up here and we can leave."

When they arrived, Celestia greeted them at the door. It was the first time in all of the years Brie had known her that Celestia looked troubled. "I'm so grateful to see you all. Please come in."

As she moved to the side to let them pass, she knelt to pet Little Sparrow. "Let's hope you are the medicine he needs, Little Sparrow." The dog licked her face excitedly.

Standing back up, she escorted them down the hall-way. As soon as Little Sparrow saw Faelan, she whined happily and raced toward him.

He stared at her, not even reaching out to pet her.

Little Sparrow would not be denied and pushed her head under his hand. Instead of relenting and petting her, he crossed his arms. She sat down and looked up at Faelan, tilting her head from side to side as if she was trying to figure him out.

Brie was frightened by the change in Faelan. He looked gaunt and his expression was hollow and lifeless.

The baby started crying in another room. Celestia immediately popped off the couch to take care of her.

"Can I go with you?" Brie asked.

She gave Brie a weak smile. "Of course."

When Brie entered the room that had been hastily converted into a nursery, she went straight to the crib and picked up the crying infant. "How has she been?"

Celestia caressed her tiny head. "The poor thing cries all the time. I haven't been able to comfort her no matter what I do."

Brie looked down sadly at the baby. "I wonder if she

misses her mother."

Celestia frowned. "I'm sure she misses them both."

Brie kissed her sweet-smelling head and began gently rocking her. "What did Faelan end up naming this little sweetie?"

Celestia looked crestfallen when she answered, "He's never given her a name."

Brie frowned. "What?"

"He refuses."

She hugged the baby tighter. "No wonder you're so unhappy."

"Brie," Celestia whispered, "I'm afraid if things don't change soon, this little girl will be an orphan."

"I promise we won't let that happen, Celestia." Remembering what Mary said, she glanced around the room. "It looks like you could use a little help with baby supplies."

"We buy things as we require them," she explained. "But, never having had a child before, we aren't really sure what else she needs."

"Don't worry. We have a small army of people who would love the opportunity to help."

Brie walked into the other room carrying the baby. The instant Faelan saw the child in her arms, he flinched and got up to leave. On his way out of the room, he told Rytsar, "Take the dog with you."

"I'm sorry," Marquis Gray stated as he watched Faelan leave. "At this point, we are at a loss."

"Don't fret," Rytsar stated confidently. "I have something in the works." He glanced at Little Sparrow. "As for her, she must stay."

"You heard what Todd said," Marquis protested.

"The boy has no idea what he needs, but I do."

They left Marquis's house not long after. On the drive home, Brie told them what she'd learned. "Faelan refuses to name the baby."

Sir frowned. "Seeing his reaction to her tonight, I can't say I'm surprised. But, it is extremely troubling."

"The boy is stubborn," Rytsar stated. "But there is *no one* more stubborn than me."

Brie trusted it was true and held desperately onto that hope.

The Plan

In the days that followed, Brie was tormented by dreams of Faelan. They had no rhyme or reason, but a sense of foreboding consumed her each morning when she awoke.

Brie was grateful when Rytsar informed them he was ready to visit Faelan again. When the three of them arrived, Rytsar walked into Marquis Gray's house without bothering to knock.

They found Faelan lying on the couch with his forearm covering his face. Little Sparrow sat beside him, her face resting on his chest. She was pushing a roll toward him with her nose.

Brie's heart caught when she remembered the story of how Little Sparrow had stolen food for Rytsar, keeping him alive in Russia. The little dog understood the seriousness of the situation and was trying to do the same thing for Faelan.

"Come with me," Rytsar ordered.

Faelan didn't move or even respond.

"Now."

Faelan croaked, "Go away."

"I'm not asking," Rytsar stated, striding over to him.

Little Sparrow stood up as Rytsar approached, wagging her tail excitedly. Rytsar patted her head. "You have done well, *Vorobyshek*."

He then grabbed Faelan's arm to pull him off the couch.

"What's this about?" Marquis Gray demanded, walking into the room.

"All will be made clear," Rytsar declared, hoisting Faelan to his feet.

Rytsar dragged him out of the room and down the hallway, ignoring his violent protests. The more Faelan cursed, the bigger the Russian's smile grew.

Rytsar pushed him through the front door and outside with everyone else following behind.

"What the hell!" Faelan snarled, shielding his face from the bright sun.

"Just wait." Rytsar crossed his arms, grinning proudly.

Brie could hear the low rumble of a muscle car approaching. When it rounded the corner she smiled, recognizing the familiar classic blue Mustang convertible.

Faelan's eyes lit up. "It can't be…"

Rytsar slapped him on the back. "But it is!"

"I never thought I would see her again," he muttered, a slow smile spreading across his face.

It was the first time Brie had seen Faelan smile since that dreadful day.

Maxim got out of the car and handed him the keys. Faelan just stood there, staring at the vehicle as if he couldn't believe it was real.

"Take her for a spin," Rytsar encouraged him.

Faelan turned to Rytsar, shaking his head in disbelief.

"I don't know what to say, Durov."

"Don't say anything." Rytsar pushed him toward the car. "Get the fuck out of here."

Faelan didn't need to be told twice. When he opened the car door, Little Sparrow jumped in uninvited and sat in the passenger seat, wagging her tail expectantly.

Faelan chuckled, then patted her on the head. "You got a problem if I take her?"

"Be my guest," Rytsar answered.

Faelan nodded to him and then told Marquis Gray and Celestia, "Don't wait for me. I've got a lot of miles to make up." His smile grew wider when the car started up and he revved the engine.

Oblivious to anything but the car, he backed out and hit the gas as he took off.

Rytsar told them, "He needed a reminder of who he once was."

Marquis nodded and watched as the Mustang sped away. "Brilliant."

"It wasn't easy to pull off," Rytsar informed him, chuckling. "The new owner wasn't willing to part with the car."

"How did you convince him?" Brie asked.

Rytsar replied sinisterly, "I made him an offer he couldn't refuse."

When her eyes widened, he laughed. "Not that kind of offer, *radost moya*. I found the same model in better condition."

"I'm certain that came at a steep price," Sir remarked.

"I'm sure," Marquis Gray agreed. "Now that you have his attention, Durov, what do you plan to do with it?"

Rytsar put his arm around Marquis Gray. "I have a proposal I'd like you to consider."

"Go on."

"I want to take the Wolf Pup with me to Russia to secure a facility for Lilly."

Brie felt the hairs rise on the back of her neck just hearing Lilly's name.

"A facility?" Marquis glanced at Sir.

Nodding to Brie, Sir answered, "The two of us have given it a lot of thought."

"Tell me more," Marquis encouraged him as they all walked back into the house.

"I want to honor Brie's desire for mercy while balancing my need to protect her from Lilly."

"And, I have the means to build a secure facility in a remote area of Russia," Rytsar explained.

"It was something about Lilly's current location at the convent that I approved of—its remoteness. There's zero chance of survival should she attempt to escape," Sir informed him.

"I see," Marquis Gray answered gravely.

Brie spoke up, "We want to give Lilly the chance to recover if it's medically possible."

"Please sit," Marquis told them, indicating they sit on the couch while he guided Celestia to sit beside him. "How do you propose to do that?"

Brie smiled, then looked at Rytsar to answer.

"I have spoken to Dr. Volkov. He has agreed to oversee her care."

"Is that the Russian doctor you spoke so highly of?" Marquis asked.

"*Da.*"

Marquis Gray sat back in his chair. After taking several moments to contemplate their plan in silence, he turned to face Sir.

"I commend you for coming up with a workable compromise."

Sir nodded.

It was high praise coming from Marquis Gray and it gave Brie confidence they were on the right path with Lilly.

"However…" Marquis glanced at Rytsar. "I do not understand what any of this has to do with Todd."

"I'm taking him to Russia with me."

"You said that." Marquis frowned. "But, putting him at greater risk is not a solution. The baby needs her father."

"Exactly," Rytsar agreed. "But the man is wasting away." He swept his hand toward Brie and Sir. "We all see it."

"What possible benefit is there to taking him out of the country?" Marquis demanded.

"I will straighten him out."

Marquis Gray's sarcastic laughter filled the room. "That's preposterous. What makes you think you will have any more success reaching him than the rest of us?"

"I'm the only one who understands his pain."

Marquis sighed heavily and did not offer a rebuttal because he knew Rytsar was right.

"The boy needs distance to be able to clear his head," Rytsar insisted.

Marquis Gray did not look convinced.

Sir leaned forward, telling him, "Durov speaks from experience."

"*Da*. The best thing my dear *mamulya* ever did was force me to attend college in America after Tatianna's death."

"You believe separating Todd from his daughter is the best thing for him—for either of them?" Marquis challenged.

Rytsar furrowed his brow. "Is he really here for her now?"

Marquis glanced at Celestia and frowned. "No, he hasn't been present since her birth."

"He cannot embrace the babe until he accepts his woman's death. Once he does that, he will realize the gift he has been given. I can get him to that point."

"How can you make such a claim?" Marquis Gray demanded.

Rytsar answered, pointing to his left eye, "The boy saved my life and the life of my friends the day he made that sacrifice. It is a debt I can never repay. I will not let him fail."

Marquis glanced at Sir. "And you support this idea?"

"Desperate times call for desperate measures."

"What about you, Brianna?" Marquis asked her.

She could not hide her growing fear from him. "If something drastic isn't done soon, the baby will have no father."

Marquis growled under his breath. "I do not care for the risk this involves."

Celestia gently put her arm on Marquis Gray's shoulder. "We are losing him."

He nodded curtly.

Marquis turned to Rytsar. "If Todd insists on joining you, I will not stop him." He let out a long sigh. "I am reminded of something I learned long ago. There are times when to save a life, you must first lose it."

Celestia looked at him sadly, nodding her agreement.

Rytsar smiled confidently. "I'm glad you see it my way."

Marquis Gray's eyes narrowed. "But if anything happens to him…"

Rytsar chuckled. "I would forfeit my life without hesitation to protect the Wolf Pup." He looked around the room. "Now that we are in agreement, I will speak with the boy when he returns."

Faelan arrived hours later. Rytsar met him outside and took him on a long walk with Little Sparrow following gleefully behind them.

Upon their return, Faelan surprised everyone with his announcement. "I feel it's best I leave for Russia, the sooner the better."

"You should think on this more," Marquis insisted. "You don't have the luxury of making rash decisions now that you are a father, especially in your current state."

Faelan seemed offended by his assertion but mulled it over before answering. "You are right, Asher. I have been crazy with grief—in a literal sense. You and I both know it. I need a purpose I can focus on. Helping with Lilly gives me that. It will provide me with purpose while I work through the pain of Kylie's death."

"What about your baby? She needs you!" Celestia cried.

Faelan sounded remorseful when he answered. "I do not have the capacity to care for anyone right now. I'm asking for a grace period, Celestia. Will you continue to look after my daughter?"

Celestia looked distraught. "I would be happy to care for her, but I worry about the separation for her—and for you."

Faelan shook his head. "It is better she is in the arms of someone who can give her the love and attention she needs."

"If you are truly leaving, can you give me a name I can call her?" she begged.

Faelan sighed, looking in the direction of the baby's room. "Call her Grace for the time being. God knows she and I could use plenty of it."

"You are coming back, I hope?" Celestia asked with concern.

"I am not abandoning my child," he assured her. "But I hope to be a better man…a better father on my return."

She bowed her head. "Then I will pray for you to return safe and whole."

"I will never be whole again."

Celestia looked at him, her eyes filled with sympathy.

"I need to get far, far away from here," he told everyone. "But joining Kylie is not an honorable option."

He looked at Brie. "Being able to protect you from that creature? That gives me both purpose and distance."

It was the first time she had seen a spark of determination from Faelan since Kylie's death. It gave her hope for his future.

Marquis must have sensed it too, because he said, "If that is how you honestly feel, I will respect your decision."

"Thank you, Asher."

"It's settled then." Rytsar slapped Faelan on the shoulder. "Get packing. It's cold in Russia."

Brie left with Rytsar and Sir. She had a much lighter heart on the drive home, but now she had to face the idea of Rytsar leaving again.

"It seems like fate is determined to keep pulling you back to Russia," she complained softly.

Rytsar smirked, wrapping his arm around her. "Are you going to miss me, *radost moya?*"

"Of course."

Looking at Sir, he grinned. "Then I must give you a going-away present."

Cuffed

Before Rytsar left for his extended trip, he invited them over for dinner. He'd informed them that it was a formal event and requested they dress for it.

Knowing it would be the last night they saw him before he left for Russia, Brie asked if he would like her parents to babysit Hope.

"Of course not. *Moye solntse* must attend!"

Brie had assumed his goodbye gift would be a night of kinky fun, but it appeared that was not the case.

"Dinner will be at seven. Do not be late."

Just to make sure no kinkiness was involved, Brie asked, "If I happen to be late, will I be punished?"

"Your punishment will be knowing you've insulted me."

His reply left no doubt this was simply a dinner invite.

However, Brie didn't understand how serious Rytsar was about the formality of the evening until he sent Hope a sophisticated new dress. It was made of black lace ruffles with tiny pearls sewn onto the collar in a braided pattern.

After Hope's dress arrived, Sir informed Brie, "I have a new gown for you to wear tonight as well. It's waiting for you in the bedroom."

Brie grinned, giving him a graceful bow before running to the bedroom.

On the bed, she found a conservative but alluring black gown. Lying beside the gown was the long strand of white pearls Sir had given her during her training. Although these pearls had a complex history, she had never forgotten the way he'd used them the first time as her Khan. Just thinking about it had her pussy quivering in delightful remembrance.

The gown had a low, sexy back and, when Brie put it on, she noticed that rather than concealing her baby bump, the dress accentuated it. She looped the pearls once before slipping them on and let them drape down her back.

For the evening, Sir dressed in his most expensive suit. The three of them looked like the definition of elegance and sophistication as they made their way to Rytsar's home.

When Maxim answered the door, Brie was surprised to see he was dressed to the nines, as well. Incredible aromas wafted out the door, hinting at the feast they were about to enjoy.

Walking into the house, Brie spotted a man dressed in chef's clothing moving round the kitchen and realized Rytsar had hired a personal chef for the evening.

"Would you like a cocktail while you wait?" Maxim asked formally.

"Certainly." Sir smirked. "We'll have two coconut waters on the rocks and a sippy cup of apple juice."

Maxim kept a straight face and left them.

Brie glanced at the dining table and let out a little squeal. Candles ran down the center of the table, their flames reflecting the gold accents of the table settings and the beautiful crystal water goblets.

When Rytsar walked into the room, Brie's jaw dropped. He was wearing a sharp, charcoal gray business suit with a vibrant red tie and sleek, polished dress shoes. She had never seen him look quite so striking before.

"Thank you for coming," he stated in a regal voice.

Brie bowed her head.

"I must say, *moy droog*, your woman looks particularly stunning tonight."

"You're not so bad yourself," Sir replied.

Rytsar looked down at his suit. "This? It's something I had at the back of my closet."

Walking over to Hope, he held out his arms to her. "Come to me, *moye solntse*. Let me look at how beautiful you are in your pretty little dress."

Hope giggled as Rytsar lifted her into the air and twirled her around. "You look like a proper *printsessa*."

To Brie's surprise, Maxim returned, handing Sir and Brie their coconut water on ice in heavy cut crystal glasses, and then he held out a golden sippy cup to Hope. "Apple juice for the young lady."

Hope grinned as she took the shiny cup from him. Bringing it to her lips, she began sucking on it eagerly.

Brie giggled. "I never would have thought gold sippy cups were a thing."

"Only the best of the best for *moye solntse*," Rytsar stated, smiling at the little girl.

Seeing Rytsar and Sir dressed in such fine suits was like an aphrodisiac for Brie—she couldn't take her eyes off of them. It was almost as if the suits held some kind of power over her.

"What made you decide to hold such a formal dinner?" she asked, adding quickly, "Not that I'm complaining. I'm actually in awe at how handsome you both look tonight."

Rytsar gazed at her with those intense blue eyes and she felt a shiver run through her. "This is my gift to you."

Brie's heart melted as she first glanced at the chef, busy making a multi-course meal, then to the elaborately set table. Her eyes drifted to Maxim dressed in finery beside her little girl, and finally to the glass of coconut water she held in her hand—a substance Rytsar abhorred.

All of this is for me?

She met his gaze, overwhelmed by the gift. A simple thank you was not enough. "I don't know what to say, Rytsar."

"Don't say anything," he smiled. "Just enjoy the evening, *radost moya.*"

"Dinner is served," Maxim announced.

Overwhelmed with gratitude, Brie walked to the dining table with Sir. Rytsar directed her to sit at the head of the table.

She sat down with both men on either side. Rytsar insisted that Hope sit beside him.

The first course was caviar with blinis.

"This was a staple for holiday meals when I was young."

Brie picked up the small blini. It had a dollop of sour cream and a generous amount of caviar spread on top.

Rytsar waited as she took a bite.

The tiny eggs popped delightfully in her mouth as

she chewed, the saltiness of it mixing well with the sour cream and light pancake texture.

She daintily wiped her mouth with her napkin afterward, trying to keep with the formalness of the dinner. She smiled and told him, "I could eat these all day."

He chuckled, giving Hope a small spoonful of the caviar to try. She bit down on the spoon, took the bite, and then stuck out her tongue as if she didn't like it. It was adorable because her tongue was black from the caviar. When Rytsar tried to wipe it away with a napkin, Hope closed her mouth and started chewing with a quizzical expression.

"It's an acquired taste, *moye solntse*," Rytsar explained, chuckling with amusement.

The second course was a light, cold soup with a lemony tang to it. It was something both Brie and Hope enjoyed immensely.

"I remember this soup," Sir stated when he tasted it.

"Would you like me to throw my spoon at you, *moy droog?*"

Brie looked up to see Rytsar ready to sling it at Sir's face.

"I'll pass this time," Sir replied, chuckling.

Brie looked at them both, wondering what they were referencing.

Rytsar answered her unspoken question by telling her, "Your Master saved my life with this soup."

Sir smirked. "So, he threw the spoon as thanks."

Rytsar shrugged. "What can I say? I did not appreciate his efforts at the time."

Brie listened with interest, sipping the soup as Rytsar and Sir reminisced, learning more about their fascinating past with each other. She was surprised to find out that shortly after Rytsar's mother died, Sir traveled to Russia to find him, missing his last semester of college.

Rytsar admitted that he hated Sir for it at the time. "Your Master is a stubborn ass, *radost moya*."

Brie struggled not to smile.

"However, a truer brother I could not find." Rytsar held up his water goblet to him.

Sir nodded, holding up the coconut water. "The same is true of you—on both counts—old friend."

Rytsar snorted.

The next course completely surprised Brie. Instead of another Russian dish, Brie was presented with a Cloche serving dish with a silver dome.

The moment Sir lifted his, he laughed.

Curious, Brie lifted hers and was confused to see a small plate of chicken and waffles. She looked at Rytsar in amusement.

"It was the beginning for you," he answered cryptically as he secured a bib around Hope's neck.

Brie turned to Sir, amused. "What does he mean?"

Sir sat back in his chair, grinning as he stared at the dish. "Back in college, Anderson introduced me to this dish." He glanced at her. "I bet you can guess where it was made."

Brie crinkled her brows, unsure what the southern dish had to do with her.

Rytsar picked up the side of warm maple syrup on the plate and poured it all over the fried chicken and waffle, a satisfied grin on his face.

Brie followed suit when she noticed Sir doing the same.

As they ate, the two men shared humorous stories about Master Anderson back in college. Laughter filled the room as they talked about his mini bullwhip named Myrtle and how legendary he was for laying on the cowboy charm.

"Remember how the cattle man was always on the hunt for the perfect 'shoe', comrade?"

Sir snickered.

Brie quickly deduced that the shoe they were talking about had to do with women who could handle Master Anderson's enormous asset. She adored hearing the two men recount stories about their college days, many of which she had never heard before.

It made her feel a part of them somehow.

"In the end, I suppose I have Anderson to thank for meeting Brie," Sir told Rytsar.

"I suppose you're right, *moy droog.*"

When Brie was finished with her plate, Rytsar asked, "Have you figured out how this dish is related to you, *radost moya?*"

She discretely dabbed at her lips to wipe away the remaining syrup as she thought about it. Sir had mentioned she would know where it was made, and that Master Anderson had been involved somehow. Once she made the connection that it had something to do with their college years in LA, it didn't take her long to figure it out.

Tears pricked her eyes as she thought back on that moment when she met Sir for the first time at the young age of seven. "Was it the diner?"

"Yes," Sir answered with satisfaction. He leaned in to kiss her, murmuring, "You missed a spot, babygirl." Brie trembled as he licked the side of her mouth.

"And now for dessert," Rytsar announced.

Brie giggled. "I'm sorry, Rytsar, I couldn't eat another bite."

He frowned. "I hope that's not true."

Maxim presented Brie with a wrapped gift on a gold dessert plate.

Brie smiled at Rytsar as she eagerly pulled on the gold bow and opened the lid of the box. Inside were the jeweled handcuffs he had given her at the collaring ceremony.

More memories flooded her as she thought back to that night. She glanced at Sir, remembering the thrill she'd felt when he placed the collar around her neck and officially claimed her as his.

When Rytsar placed a bottle of chilled vodka beside the cuffs, Brie looked at him with a bemused grin. "You know I can't drink."

"Vodka makes *everything* taste better," he replied in a seductive tone.

Rytsar turned to Hope and cleaned her face before taking off the bib and handing her to Maxim. "She loves it if you rock her on the horse. And, if all else fails, turn on her grandfather's violin music and dance with her. She never tires of it."

"Yes, *gospodin.*" Maxim took Hope from him and nodded to Brie before leaving the room.

"And then there were three..." Sir stated.

Brie's heart skipped a beat when she realized that her kinky wish was about to come true.

Rytsar stood up, holding out his hand to Brie. "Would you care to join us in the bedroom, *radost moya?*"

Brie picked up the handcuffs before taking his hand. "If it pleases you," she answered demurely.

Rytsar glanced at Sir who grabbed the bottle of vodka.

"It most certainly does."

Once in the bedroom, Brie was ordered to undress both men. She took her time, enjoying the sensual nature of the process—the soft feel of the silk ties as she undid the knots and slipped them through the men's collars, removing the tailored jackets before slowly unbuttoning their shirts one button at a time.

Brie always found it erotic when she exposed their bare chests, running her hands lightly over their firm muscles.

The shoes and socks came next. Then she undid their belts. The clinking sound of the metal as she unbuckled them always gave her a thrill.

Her movements were unhurried and reverent as she removed each piece of clothing, giving each Dom her full attention.

When they were both naked, Rytsar commanded her to give him the handcuffs. She did so eagerly, curious as to how he would use them. To her surprise, he put one of the cuffs around his wrist and the other around Sir's.

"What will you do?" he asked with a smirk.

Brie's eyes widened when she realized they were giving her free rein over their bodies. This was the ultimate power play—one where she was in control of the scene.

Normally, as the submissive, she was the one naked while her Dom remained dressed. Enjoying this unique dynamic, she chose to leave her clothes on for the scene.

Looking at their hard cocks, her eyes gravitated to the bottle of vodka. She picked it up, noting how cold it was, and giggled inwardly as she approached them.

Kneeling on the floor between the two men, Brie opened the bottle of Zyr, enjoying the pop of the cork.

Looking up at Rytsar, she purred. "You said everything tastes better with vodka…"

"I did." His eyes burned with lust for her.

Brie held the neck of the bottle above his shaft and let it slowly pour down. She heard his sharp intake of breath and smiled, imagining the shock the chilled vodka would provide.

Opening her lips, she took his shaft into her warm mouth and heard him groan in pleasure as she moved up and down his cock at a leisurely pace.

Not wanting to ignore Sir, she turned and did the same to him, looking up at his face demurely as she poured the ice-cold vodka down his shaft. He grunted at the shocking cold, then threw his head back the moment she took his cock into her mouth.

Her pussy grew wet as she watched their expressions while she tortured and teased their shafts with the chilled liquor.

Directing them to the expansive bed, she told them to lie down as she removed her shoes and slipped out of her panties.

Once Brie had joined them on the bed, she placed the cold bottle between Rytsar's legs, resting it against his ballsack.

He let out a low growl, responding to the intensity of it. While she let him "chill", Brie devoted her attention to Sir, leaving kisses and bites up and down his body. Needing the fullness of his shaft inside her, Brie lifted the skirt of her dress and straddled him, descending onto his rock-hard shaft.

"*Radost moya…*" Rytsar groaned as he watched her.

Taking pity on him, she removed the bottle and wasn't surprised to see the effect the cold had had on his shaft.

But that was part of her wicked plan.

With Sir's cock still deep in her pussy, she leaned over and started licking and sucking on Rytsar's cock, making it spring back to life. It didn't take long before it was hard and ready for her.

She disengaged from Sir to straddle Rytsar, encasing him in her warmth while she teased Sir's shaft.

She did this several times, the seductive challenge of the ice-cold vodka and her warm mouth making both men crazy for her.

Greedy for their dual attention, Brie slipped the material of her dress off her shoulders, exposing her full breasts to them. She lay between them, resting her head on their cuffed hands, and told them to suck on her breasts while she wrapped her hands around their shafts and stroked them at the same time.

It was gloriously sensual to feel the tug on her nipples while feeling the strength of their erections as she played with them. It was a heady experience, and Brie felt the first flutters of an impending orgasm.

However, she wasn't ready to give in to it yet, anxious to be pounded by both men.

Brie asked Rytsar to lie on his back with his head near the edge of the mattress while Sir stood at the side of the bed. She then leaned against the bed, her breasts dangling above Rytsar's mouth while she begged Sir to fuck her.

The Russian began sucking on one nipple while pinching the other between his fingers, making Brie moan in pleasure.

Sir lifted the material of her dress with his free hand, exposing her naked ass. He slapped it, the sexy sound of the contact echoing through the room.

Brie let out an excited cry as Sir plowed into her, possessing her with his cock and showing no mercy after her extended teasing. It didn't take long before the flutters of her climax became powerful contractions as she came forcefully around his shaft.

Sir pulled out, slapping her ass again, demanding to change places.

Brie happily agreed, watching in pleasure as the men navigated exchanging positions still bound in the cuffs.

When they were ready, Brie leaned over Sir. He immediately grasped her right breast in his free hand and began sucking hard on the left. The aggressive manner in which he played with her turned her on even more.

Rytsar grasped her waist with one hand and thrust into her, stealing away her breath with the depth of his penetration. He released her waist and fisted her long hair, pulling her head back. "Now, you will experience my final gift to you, *radost moya*."

Brie closed her eyes, willingly giving her body over to his desire.

Rytsar's strokes were deep and demanding, making her forget everything except the pleasurable tugging on her nipples as Sir played with them.

When Rytsar ramped up his thrusts, the dual stimulation quickly became too much. Brie moaned in extreme pleasure as she came around his shaft, milking it hard with her inner muscles.

Rytsar let out a roar as he pulled out of her, too close to coming.

Acting on her own desire, Brie knelt on the floor. Both men understood what she wanted without being asked and stood on either side of her, still connected by the cuffs. She took their cocks in her hands and looked up at them as she stroked their shafts.

Opening her mouth in invitation, Brie was soon rewarded with the warmth of their come as they covered her with their seed.

It was a wholly possessive feeling to have both men come at the same time, accentuating the power she always felt when she was on her knees.

On the walk home, Brie reflected on the evening. Every detail of the night had been a carefully orchestrated gift to her.

With each dish, Rytsar had opened up a little more about himself to her. From the appetizer, which was a part of his childhood, to the soup that had started a discussion about Rytsar's past history with Sir. They led up to the main dish which uncovered the beginning of Brie and Sir.

All of it had been for her...

However, the greatest gift had been Rytsar giving her free reign over him tonight.

Brie understood the significance of that gift coming from the burly, dominant Russian, and she was profoundly humbled by it.

It was the ultimate act of trust.

This Moment

B rie woke up to Sir calling out from the bathroom. "What is the meaning of this?"

She got up and ran to the bathroom. "What's wrong?"

Sir lifted the toilet seat with one hand while pointing at the rim with the other. Brie looked down and was shocked to see a foiled square with a smiley on it staring up at her in the same exact position she had placed it in Rytsar's bathroom all those months ago.

She put a hand to her lips, giggling. "I guess Rytsar knows I had something to do with Master Anderson's prank."

Sir's hand slipped and the lid fell with a loud clank. Brie's eyes grew wide as she quickly lifted the lid and was horrified to see the fart bomb starting to grow.

"Oh no, oh no, oh no!" she cried, grabbing it by the corner and running as fast as she could toward the front door. In her haste, she fumbled with the lock and whimpered as the bomb continued to expand.

Oblivious to her naked state, Brie flung open the door and threw the fart bomb away. It skidded across the porch, hitting the side wall where it stopped. She watched as it filled up until it made a satisfying pop.

When Brie caught a whiff of the obnoxious smell, she started to laugh uncontrollably. Sliding down the frame of the door, she sat there, laughing so hard her sides hurt.

That's when one of their neighbors jogged past. The woman did a double-take when she noticed Brie was naked.

Scooching on her ass back into the house, Brie quickly kicked the door shut, still overcome with laughter.

Rytsar had one more gift to give before leaving…

Brie realized Master Anderson was right. There were times when a practical joke was a sincere expression of love.

Sir stared at her with an amused expression, shaking his head.

"Oh, he got me good…" she said, wiping the tears from her eyes.

Sir chuckled, helping Brie to her feet. "What *will* you tell the neighbors?"

Later that day, Mary called. Brie could hear the elation in her voice. "Hey, Stinks!

She pressed the phone against her cheek, thrilled to hear that kind of excitement from Mary.

"You'll never guess where I am."

Brie laughed. "I don't have a clue."

"You have to guess."

She took a moment to come up with something clever. "You're in Vegas, married to an Elvis impersonator?"

Mary actually laughed. "Not bad, Stinks, but you're wrong."

"Okay, then. Where are you?"

Mary threw her for a loop when she answered, "I'm staying at Lea's apartment."

Brie snorted. "Why?"

"Greg is out for blood."

Chills suddenly paralyzed Brie where she stood. "What's happened, Mary?"

"It's all hush, hush, but Greg caught wind that you'll be receiving a proposal in the next day or two."

Although Brie was excited at the prospect, she was extremely concerned for Mary. "What about you?"

"Don't worry about me. I just need to keep clear of the asshole while I watch his entire world burn to the ground."

"You could stay with us."

She snorted. "Ah, no. If I were to be seen anywhere near you right now, it would be considered high treason."

"I'm so sorry, Mary."

"Don't be sorry," she reprimanded Brie. "This is everything we've been working for."

"But, it comes at such a great cost to you."

"Listen, Brie. I have been controlled by that fucker all of my life. Everything that I've done to help you, I knew Greg saw it as a slap across his face. I understand there may be consequences, and I fully accept them. For the first time in my life, my eyes are open and my actions are my own."

The power in Mary's voice was inspiring.

"You're going to be big, Brie. Mark my words. Everyone will know your name."

"That doesn't mean anything to me unless I know you're safe."

She laughed. "You're so unprofessional, Stinks. In a dog-eat-dog world, you're like a fluffy bunny. You're lucky you've got a weasel like me protecting your back."

"You're not a weasel, Mary. You're a freaking eagle with razor-sharp talons that rip and restrain your prey while you eat them alive."

"Oh yeah, I like that. Hey, before I let you go, I have another juicy tidbit for you."

"Fine. I'll bite."

"I visited Celestia with a load of baby shit. She told me Todd received a letter in the mail. You'll never guess who it's from."

"You're killing me, Mary," Brie chuckled.

"It's from Trevor's mother."

"Trevor?" she asked, before remembering it was the name of the boy Faelan had killed in the car accident. "Oh God, that's the last thing he needs."

"I advised her to burn it, but Marquis won't let her."

Brie desperately prayed that whatever was in the letter wouldn't derail Faelan when he returned to the States.

Brie struggled to fall asleep that night.

Rather than fight it, she opened her eyes and stared at Sir, who was sleeping soundly.

She was struck by how incredibly handsome he was,

lying there peaceful and still.

The immense love she felt for him suddenly bubbled up inside of her. It was so intense that she struggled not to caress his face.

Brie didn't want to wake him, but the urge proved too much and she lightly grazed her hand against his cheek, thrilled at the connection she felt.

He opened his eyes, staring straight into hers.

For a moment, Brie felt guilty knowing she had just woken him in the middle of the night.

But a smile spread across his face. "Hello."

She swooned just hearing his voice.

"What was that for?" he asked.

Brie could hardly contain her love when she told him, "I saw you lying there and was so overcome with emotion, I just had to touch you."

His smile broadened. "Really?"

She nodded. "I'm sorry for waking you."

He pulled her against him. "I'm not."

Brie sighed in contentment as he spooned against her, his hand resting on her belly.

They lay together in the dark, in comfortable silence, feeling their baby's movements.

This is heaven.

Brie savored this moment of pure joy.

Whatever tomorrow might bring, she had this moment in time no one could ever steal from her.

I hope you enjoyed *Her Sweet Surrender!*

Do not worry about Faelan, my dear readers. His friends will not fail him, and his love for Kylie and their child will become his strength.

Reviews mean the world to me!

I truly appreciate you taking the time to review Her Sweet Surrender.

TWO BOOKS COMING UP NEXT!
Preorder Now

The Ties That Bind
The next book in the Brie's Submission series!

When you are part of the Submissive Training Center, you are never alone.

A fateful trip to Russia is in Brie's future after the birth of their second child. In a world of uncertainty, the passionate connection between a Dom and his submissive remains true.

While the community bands together to help one of their own, a surprising secret is revealed—one that will have life-changing consequences.

And

The Cowboy's Secret
A standalone novel in the Unleashed Series

Master Anderson – The cowboy with a heart of gold.

Ready to prove himself as a young man, Brad Anderson heads back to Colorado, leaving LA and his trusted friends behind.

With a good head for business and his talent with the bullwhip, Brad is determined to leave his mark in the business world—and in the bedroom.

His life will change once his secret is unleashed.

~~~~~~~

Want to start at the beginning when Sir, Rytsar and Master Anderson first met?

Begin with **Sir's Rise** the 1st book in the
Rise of the Dominants Trilogy

~~~~~~~

BONUS CONTENT!

Bonus 1 – Grab the exclusive story of Lea's First Day at the Submissive Training Center at BookFunnel.

Bonus 2 – Enjoy this beautiful scene between Brie and Sir that I wrote years ago. It never made it into the series, but I love it so much I wanted to share it with you here so it will never be lost!

A Condor's Birthday

By Red Phoenix

B rie had been planning Sir's thirty-fifth birthday for months even though he'd insisted on no parties and no presents.

"Birthdays are for the young," he'd declared when Brie first mentioned wanting to throw him a party.

"Just like Christmas?" she pressed, knowing how he felt about the holiday.

"Similar, yes."

"Well, I don't agree, Sir."

He smirked. "Why am I not surprised?"

Ever since that conversation, Brie had kept her plans under wraps, hoping Sir would forgive her when she surprised him on his special day…

As she stood with Sir on the beach, watching the sun as it began to set over the ocean, Brie smiled to herself.

Sir took her hand and lifted it to his lips. "This is nice. A perfect way to end the day."

"Your thirty-fifth *birthday*," she reminded him.

He shrugged. "A day like any other."

"Not to me, Sir."

Sir chuckled. "At least you respected my wishes and did not embarrass me with presents or cake."

"No presents or cake," she agreed, glancing nervously behind her.

"I would have had to punish you if you'd disobeyed me. Thankfully you are a good and obedient sub." He put his finger under her chin, tilting her head up to kiss her.

Brie melted as he gave her a long, passionate kiss. When he pulled away, she gave him a half-smile, feeling even more anxious.

Would he still feel that way in a couple of minutes?

Trying not to give away her big surprise, Brie replied lightly, "You know how you say we are condors?"

"Of course."

"Well, thirty-five is a significant year for a condor."

"What does that have to do with me?"

As if on cue, there was a loud squawk behind them.

Brie grinned as she watched Sir's expression change as he turned around and saw the large California condor and its mate being held by their handlers. He stared at them, a stunned look on his face, as he took in the magnificent bird flapping its nine-foot-wide wingspan.

"Meet AC-4, Sir. He's a thirty-five-year-old condor, just like you," she explained.

"Wow," Sir murmured, awed by the creature.

"They are releasing him today," Brie gushed.

"This is incredible…"

"I'm so glad you think so!" she cried excitedly. "Because I invited a few of your friends to join us."

The two handlers parted to reveal the large crowd of people who had gathered on the beach to witness the momentous release—including the entire staff of the

Submissive Training Center.

Sir looked at Brie, raising an eyebrow. "You are a *very* bad girl."

Brie didn't miss the glint in his eye.

While reporters flashed their cameras, the two handlers counted to three before letting the birds go at the same time.

The two giant birds flapped their mighty wings, pushing themselves up into the air.

It was truly an extraordinary sight, the two massive condors circling each other as they rose higher and higher in the sky, calling to each other—finally *free*.

The crowd clapped and cheered wildly, Sir among them.

"Happy birthday, Sir!" she cried, wrapping her arms around him as everyone began singing "Happy Birthday" to him.

Brie suspected there might be a spanking in her future, but she didn't mind one little bit…

If you would like to donate to the California Condor recovery efforts, go here:

Ventana Wildlife Society

www.ventanaws.org

COMING NEXT

The Ties That Bind
Book 22 of the Brie's Submission Series
Available for Preorder

The Cowboy's Secret
A complete standalone novel in
The Unleashed Series
Available for Preorder

Reviews mean the world to me!

I truly appreciate you taking the time to review
Her Sweet Surrender.

If you could leave a review on both Goodreads and the
site where you purchased this eBook from, I would be so
grateful. Sincerely, ~Red

You can begin the journey of Sir, Rytsar and Master
Anderson when they first met with *Sir's Rise* the 1st book
in the *Rise of the Dominants Series*!

Start reading NOW!

ABOUT THE AUTHOR

Over Two Million readers have enjoyed Red's stories

Red Phoenix – USA Today Bestselling Author
Winner of 8 Readers' Choice Awards

Hey Everyone!

I'm Red Phoenix, an author who also happens to be a submissive in real life. I wrote the Brie's Submission series because I wanted people everywhere to know just how much fun BDSM can be.

There is a huge cast of characters who are part of Brie's journey. The further you read into the story the more you learn about each one. I hope you grow to love Brie and the gang as much as I do.

They've become like family.

When I'm not writing, you can find me online with readers.

I heart my fans! ~Red

To find out more visit my Website

redphoenixauthor.com

Follow Me on BookBub

bookbub.com/authors/red-phoenix

Newsletter: Sign up

redphoenixauthor.com/newsletter-signup

Facebook: AuthorRedPhoenix

Twitter: @redphoenix69

Instagram: RedPhoenixAuthor

I invite you to join my reader Group!

facebook.com/groups/539875076052037

SIGN UP FOR MY NEWSLETTER
HERE FOR THE LATEST RED
PHOENIX UPDATES

FOLLOW ME ON INSTAGRAM
INSTAGRAM.COM/REDPHOENIXAUTHOR

SALES, GIVEAWAYS, NEW
RELEASES, PREORDER LINKS, AND
MORE!
SIGN UP HERE
REDPHOENIXAUTHOR.COM/NEWSLETTER-
SIGNUP

Red Phoenix is the author of:

Brie's Submission Series:
Teach Me #1
Love Me #2
Catch Me #3
Try Me #4
Protect Me #5
Hold Me #6
Surprise Me #7
Trust Me #8
Claim Me #9
Enchant Me #10
A Cowboy's Heart #11
Breathe with Me #12
Her Russian Knight #13
Under His Protection #14
Her Russian Returns #15
In Sir's Arms #16
Bound by Love #17
Tied to Hope #18
Hope's First Christmas #19
Secrets of the Heart #20
Her Sweet Surrender #21

*You can also purchase the AUDIO BOOK **Versions**

Also part of the Submissive Training Center world:

Rise of the Dominates Trilogy
Sir's Rise #1
Master's Fate #2
The Russian Reborn #3

Captain's Duet
Safe Haven #1
Destined to Dominate #2

The Russian Unleashed #1
The Cowboy's Secret #2

Other Books by Red Phoenix

Blissfully Undone
* Available in eBook and paperback

(Snowy Fun—Two people find themselves snowbound
in a cabin where hidden love can flourish, taking one
couple on a sensual journey into ménage à trois)

———————————

His Scottish Pet: Dom of the Ages
* Available in eBook and paperback

Audio Book: *His Scottish Pet: Dom of the Ages*

(Scottish Dom—A sexy Dom escapes to Scotland in the
late 1400s. He encounters a waif who has the potential to
free him from his tragic curse)

———————————

The Erotic Love Story of Amy and Troy
* Available in eBook and paperback

(Sexual Adventures—True love reigns, but fate continually throws Troy and Amy into the arms of others)

eBooks

Varick: The Reckoning

(Savory Vampire—A dark, sexy vampire story. The hero navigates the dangerous world he has been thrust into with lusty passion and a pure heart)

Keeper of the Wolf Clan (Keeper of Wolves, #1)

(Sexual Secrets—A virginal werewolf must act as the clan's mysterious Keeper)

The Keeper Finds Her Mate (Keeper of Wolves, #2)

(Second Chances—A young she-wolf must choose between old ties or new beginnings)

The Keeper Unites the Alphas (Keeper of Wolves, #3)

(Serious Consequences—The young she-wolf is captured by the rival clan)

Boxed Set: Keeper of Wolves Series (Books 1-3)

(Surprising Secrets—A secret so shocking it will rock Layla's world. The young she-wolf is put in a position of being able to save her werewolf clan or becoming the reason for its destruction)

Socrates Inspires Cherry to Blossom

(Satisfying Surrender—A mature and curvaceous woman becomes fascinated by an online Dom who has much to teach her)

By the Light of the Scottish Moon

(Saving Love—Two lost souls, the Moon, a werewolf, and a death wish…)

In 9 Days

(Sweet Romance—A young girl falls in love with the new student, nicknamed "the Freak")

---

9 Days and Counting

(Sacrificial Love—The sequel to *In 9 Days* delves into the emotional reunion of two longtime lovers)

And Then He Saved Me

(Saving Tenderness—When a young girl tries to kill
herself, a man of great character intervenes with a love
that heals)

Play With Me at Noon

(Seeking Fulfillment—A desperate wife lives out her
fantasies by taking five different men in five days)

Connect with Red on Substance B

Substance B is a platform for independent authors to directly connect with their readers. Please visit Red's Substance B page where you can:

- Sign up for Red's newsletter
- Send a message to Red
- See all platforms where Red's books are sold

Visit Substance B today to learn more about your favorite independent authors.